Honey Tanberry

Lunatic, egotistical, often sad...she loves drama, but she knows how to present herself as charming, put together, and very sweet.
15 years old

Born in Kitnor
Mum: Charlotte
Dad: Greg

Coco Tanberry

...ipper, always full of energy, she loves adventures and nature.
12 years old

Born in Kitnor
Mum: Charlotte
Dad: Greg

Summer Tanberry

Calm, confident, pretty, and popular, she takes dance extremely seriously.
13 years old

Identical twin of Skye
Born in Kitnor
Mum: Charlotte
Dad: Greg

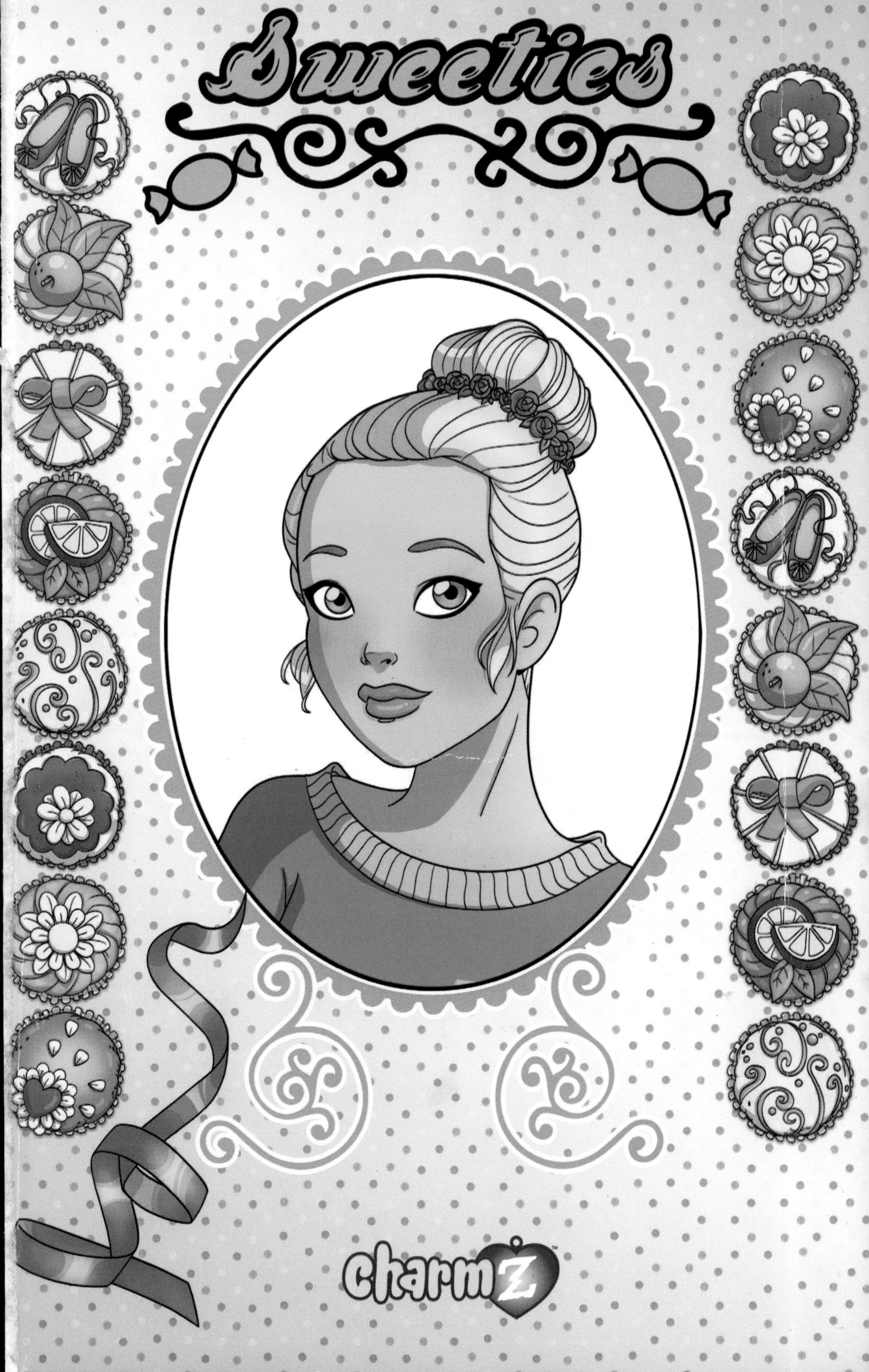
Sweeties
charmZ

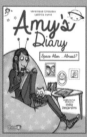

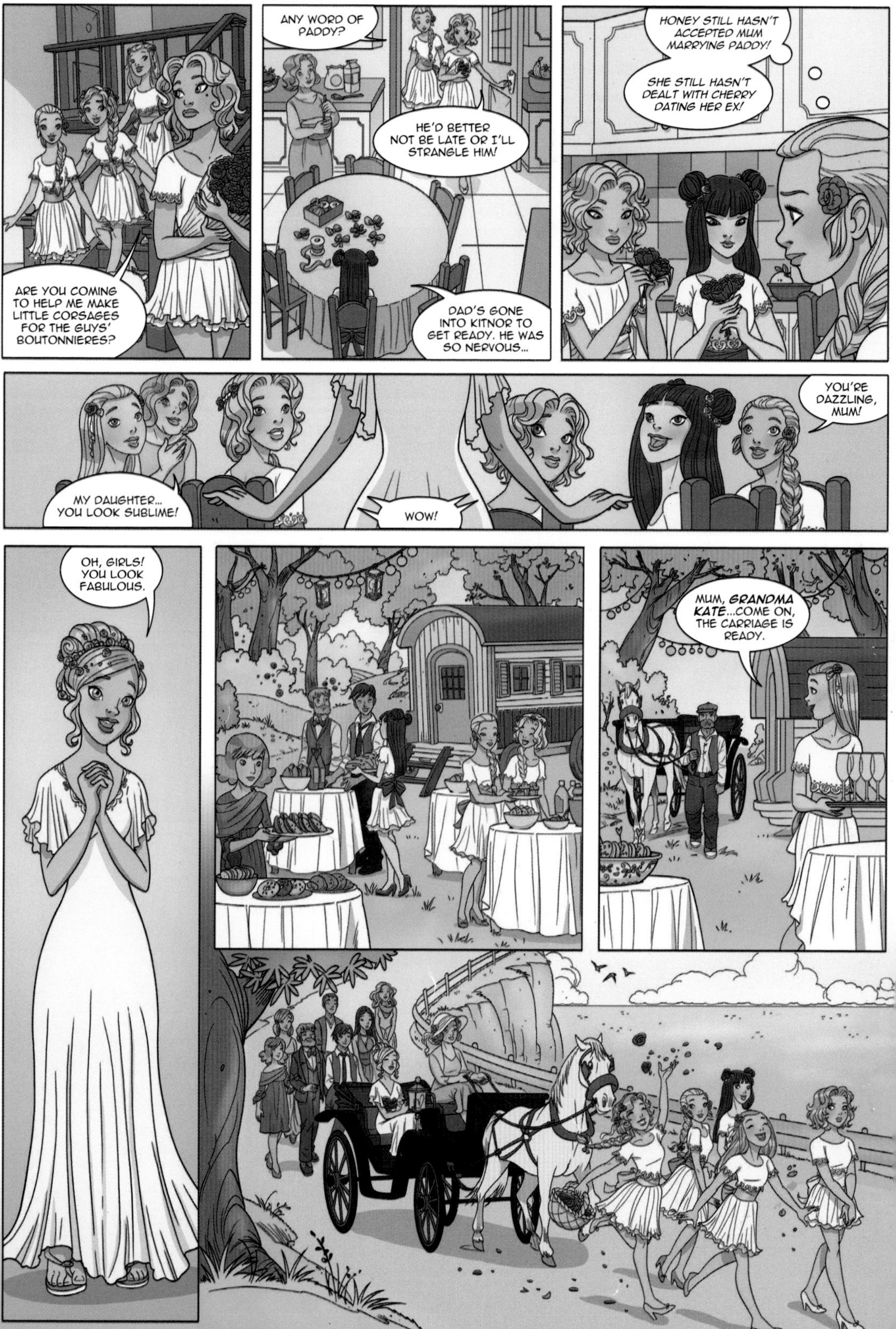
ARE YOU COMING TO HELP ME MAKE LITTLE CORSAGES FOR THE GUYS' BOUTONNIERES?
ANY WORD OF PADDY?
HE'D BETTER NOT BE LATE OR I'LL STRANGLE HIM!
DAD'S GONE INTO KITNOR TO GET READY. HE WAS SO NERVOUS...
HONEY STILL HASN'T ACCEPTED MUM MARRYING PADDY!
SHE STILL HASN'T DEALT WITH CHERRY DATING HER EX!
MY DAUGHTER... YOU LOOK SUBLIME!
WOW!
YOU'RE DAZZLING, MUM!
OH, GIRLS! YOU LOOK FABULOUS.
MUM, GRANDMA KATE...COME ON, THE CARRIAGE IS READY.

Previously in Sweeties

Cherry Costello and her father, chocolatier Paddy, move in with Paddy's girlfriend, Charlotte and her four daughters: Honey, Summer, Skye, and Coco. Right off the bat, Cherry offends the oldest daughter Honey by catching her boyfriend, Shay's eye. While Honey and Shay's relationship deteriorates, Cherry and Shay grow close and Paddy and Charlotte get engaged. Love is in the air.

Later, Skye has been having strange dreams of a Roma gentleman from the past. Meanwhile, her friend Alfie is acting strange, due to his feelings for her identical twin sister, Summer. Skye must help her friend navigate his broken heart, as her sister is going out with Aaron Jones. Meanwhile, Skye digs into the past to discover the haunting truth of the long lost romance of her ghostly suitor.

SWEETIES #2
"Summer Coco"

Based on the novels from the series "The Chocolate Box Girls" by Cathy Cassidy, first published by Puffin Books (The Penguin Group, London) The Chocolate Box Girls Summer's Dream © 2013 by Cathy Cassidy. The Chocolate Box Girls Coco Caramel ©2014 by Cathy Cassidy. Comics originally published in French as *Les filles au chocolat tome 3 "Cœur Mandarine"* © Jungle! 2016 and *tome 4 "Cœur Coco"* © Jungle! 2016
www.editions-jungle.com
All rights reserved. Used under license.
English translation and other material © 2019 by Charmz.
All rights reserved.

CATHY CASSIDY — Original Story
VÉRONIQUE GRISSEAUX — Comics Adaptation
RAYMOND SÉBASTIEN — Character Designer
CLAUDIA FORCELLONI of Yellowhale — Cover Artist
CLAUDIA FORCELLONI and MARCO FORCELLONI of Yellowhale — Artists
DRAC and REIKO of Yellowhale — Colorists
WILSON RAMOS JR. — Letterer
JOE JOHNSON — Translation
JAYJAY JACKSON — Production
KARR ANTUNES — Editorial Intern
JEFF WHITMAN — Assistant Managing Editor
JIM SALICRUP
Editor-In-Chief

Special thanks to LAUREN MUHLHEIM, Psy.D., FAED, CEDS-S, and FLORA BOFFY

Charmz is an imprint of Papercutz.
Papercutz.com

PB ISBN: 978-1-62991-837-2
HC ISBN: 978-1-62991-838-9

Charmz books may be purchased for business or promotional use.
For information on bulk purchases please contact Macmillan
Corporate and Premium Sales Department at
(800) 221-7945 x5442

Printed in India
February 2019

Distributed by Macmillan
First Charmz Printing

ONE DAY I'LL BECOME A BALLERINA...

EXMOOR Dance Studios

I'LL DANCE THE PART OF GISELLE OR COPPÉLIA OR JULIET...

THEY'RE SO CUTE! I USED TO BE JUST LIKE THEM ONCE.

I WAS GOOD. I DANCED CENTER STAGE AT EVERY RECITAL...NOT LIKE **SKYE**, MY TWIN SISTER!

AND ONE AND TWO...PLIÉ...

HEE HEE HEE!

SKYE, STOP CLOWNING AROUND! DANCE IS SERIOUS STUFF!

SHE ALWAYS MADE FUN OF ME WHENEVER I WATCHED THE DVD OF BILLY ELLIOT OVER AND OVER. AND THEN EVERYTHING FELL APART. DAD LEFT US TWO YEARS AGO. SKYE STOPPED BALLET CLASS--

WHEN SHE TOLD ME SHE ONLY DANCED BECAUSE I WANTED TO... I FELT STRANDED!

IT WAS LIKE SHE'D SLAPPED MY FACE! BUT MY WORST NIGHTMARE WAS THE DAY OF THE AUDITION FOR ADMISSION TO THE ROYAL BALLET SCHOOL...

DAD ARRIVED LATE TO TAKE ME. I WAS SICK WITH NERVES...AND...

I'D MESSED UP A ONCE-IN-A-LIFETIME OPPORTUNITY!

SINCE THEN, A SAD, SOUR VOICE WHISPERED INSIDE MY HEAD: **"YOU'D NEVER HAVE MADE IT ANYWAY."** I BRUSH THE VOICE ASIDE, ALTHOUGH I CAN'T EVER QUITE FORGET IT!

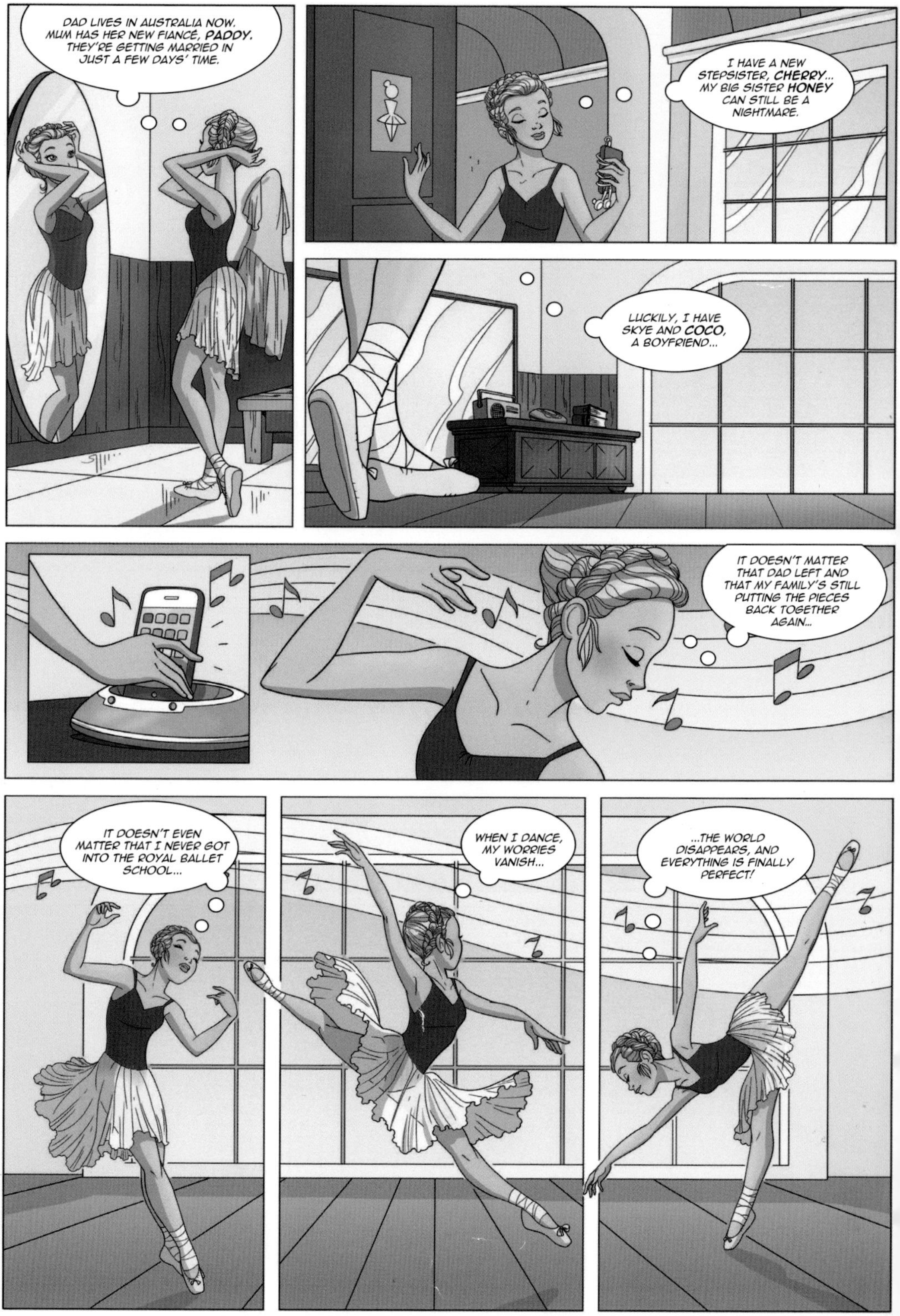
DAD LIVES IN AUSTRALIA NOW. MUM HAS HER NEW FIANCÉ, **PADDY**. THEY'RE GETTING MARRIED IN JUST A FEW DAYS' TIME.
I HAVE A NEW STEPSISTER, **CHERRY**... MY BIG SISTER **HONEY** CAN STILL BE A NIGHTMARE.
LUCKILY, I HAVE SKYE AND **COCO**, A BOYFRIEND...
IT DOESN'T MATTER THAT DAD LEFT AND THAT MY FAMILY'S STILL PUTTING THE PIECES BACK TOGETHER AGAIN...
IT DOESN'T EVEN MATTER THAT I NEVER GOT INTO THE ROYAL BALLET SCHOOL...
WHEN I DANCE, MY WORRIES VANISH...
...THE WORLD DISAPPEARS, AND EVERYTHING IS FINALLY PERFECT!

I DON'T LIKE THIS DRESS. I LOOK BIGGER THAN I REALLY AM!

SUMMER! CAN YOU HELP ME WITH MY HAIR?

THE WEDDING DAY...

WE LOOK OKAY, DON'T WE? FOR BRIDESMAIDS!

NOT A NYLON RUFFLE IN SIGHT, BUT...YOU DON'T THINK THE DRESS MAKES ME LOOK... TOO CURVY?

TOO CURVY? NO WAY, SUMMER! YOU'RE REALLY SLIM! BESIDES, WE'RE MEANT TO HAVE CURVES.

THAT'S PART OF GROWING UP!

WHEN I LOOK IN THE MIRROR THESE DAYS, IT DOESN'T EVEN LOOK LIKE ME!

WELL, IT IS, AND IT'S ME TOO... WE'RE IDENTICAL TWINS, REMEMBER!

SHOULD I MAKE A FLOWER GARLAND FOR HUMBUG'S COLLAR?

OR WOULD SHE JUST EAT IT, DO YOU THINK?

SHE'LL EAT IT, SILLY! ÷HEE HEE HEE!÷

OKAY, LET'S GO GIVE A HAND DOWNSTAIRS!

Sweeties

SUMMER COCO

Story by
Cathy Cassidy
Written by
Véronique Grisseaux
Art by Claudia & Marco Forcelloni

charmz
NEW YORK

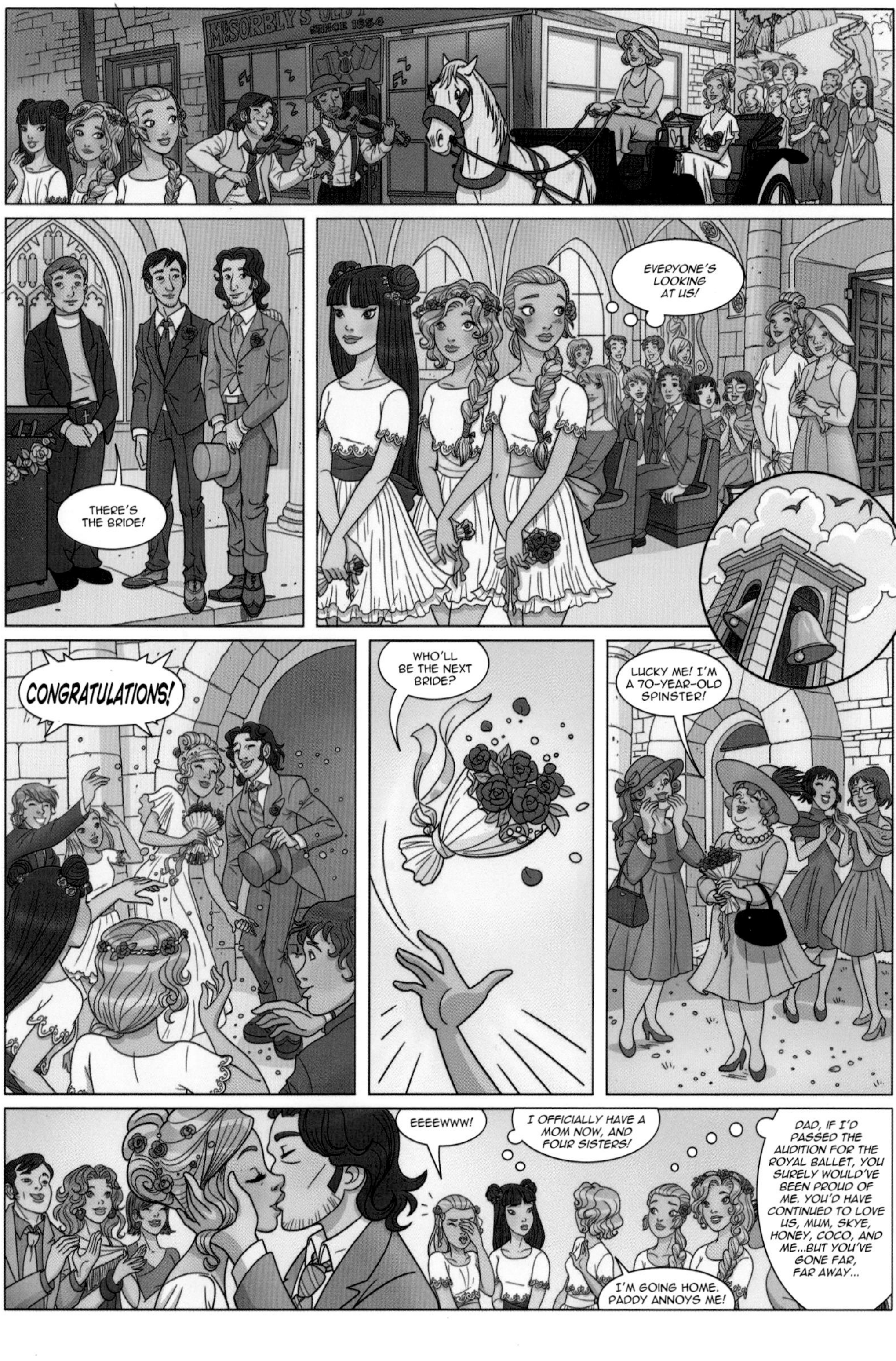
McSORBLY'S OLD
SINCE 1854
THERE'S THE BRIDE!
EVERYONE'S LOOKING AT US!
CONGRATULATIONS!
WHO'LL BE THE NEXT BRIDE?
LUCKY ME! I'M A 70-YEAR-OLD SPINSTER!
EEEEWWW!
I OFFICIALLY HAVE A MOM NOW, AND FOUR SISTERS!
I'M GOING HOME. PADDY ANNOYS ME!
DAD, IF I'D PASSED THE AUDITION FOR THE ROYAL BALLET, YOU SURELY WOULD'VE BEEN PROUD OF ME. YOU'D HAVE CONTINUED TO LOVE US, MUM, SKYE, HONEY, COCO, AND ME...BUT YOU'VE GONE FAR, FAR AWAY...

A LITTLE LATER...

COOL WEDDING. I LIKE YOUR DRESS, SUMMER!

AS CLINGY AS EVER, ALFIE!

HEY! I'M HERE. I JUST ARRIVED!

AARON!

AARON JONES IS THE CUTEST BOY IN MIDDLE SCHOOL. EVERY GIRL IN MY YEAR HAS BEEN CRUSHING ON HIM. AND HE CHOSE ME.

WOW! NICE DRESS! IT REALLY SHOWS OFF YOUR FIGURE!

THAT'S A GOOD THING! HAVE YOU EATEN YET?

THAT'S ALL YOU'RE HAVING?

SALAD'S GOOD FOR MY FIGURE!

I WASN'T HUNGRY... MY TUMMY'S ALL BUTTERFLIES!...

IT LOOKS LIKE HONEY CAN'T STAND MUM AND PADDY'S WEDDING. SHE'S STILL MAD AT DAD FOR LEAVING US!

LATER THAT EVENING...

YOU'RE THE PRETTIEST GIRL I'VE EVER DATED!

AROUND ONE A.M....

ARE YOU AND AARON IN LOVE?

I DON'T KNOW. IT'S STILL EARLY.

IT'S BEEN FOUR MONTHS. YOU MUST HAVE SOME IDEA.

DO YOU THINK ABOUT HIM ALL THE TIME?

IT'S COMPLICATED...AARON'S BEEN OUT WITH LOTS OF GIRLS. I WORRY HE'LL MOVE ON, FIND SOMEONE HE LIKES BETTER...

HE WON'T. HE'S CRAZY ABOUT YOU, ANYONE CAN SEE THAT!

DO YOU THINK A BOY WILL FEEL THAT WAY ABOUT ME SOME DAY?

OF COURSE!

GREAT PARTY LAST NIGHT, EH?

AREN'T YOU TWO SUPPOSED TO BE ON YOUR HONEYMOON AFTER THE WEDDING?

I HAVE A SURPRISE FOR YOU. IT'S MY WEDDING GIFT!

A TRIP TO THE LAND OF THE COCOA BEAN!

THREE WEEKS IN PERU! IT'S WONDERFUL, BUT WE CAN'T LEAVE SO SOON...

IT'S ALL ARRANGED. YOU'LL LEAVE THE LAST WEEK OF JULY.

I'LL STAY HERE AND SEE TO EVERYTHING, THE GIRLS, THE B&B. PADDY HAS HIRED AN ASSISTANT FOR THE CHOCOLATE BUSINESS...

YOU WERE IN ON THIS?

YES, WE'LL INVEST IN EQUITABLY SOURCED COCOA BEANS. THIS TRIP WILL COMBINE THE PRACTICAL AND PLEASURE!

..AND WE'LL KEEP AN EYE ON THE FILM CREW USING TANGLEWOOD AS THEIR BASE!

THAT AFTERNOON...

100 RELEVÉS EVERY DAY TO KEEP MY FEET AND ANKLES STRONG...IT'S MY DAILY TORTURE.

HI!

HEY, WHAT'S UP? I DIDN'T EXPECT TO SEE YOU HERE!

TO THINK THAT *JODIE* FAILED THE ENTRANCE EXAMINATION AT THE ROYAL BALLET SCHOOL LIKE I DID. THE PANEL SAID JODIE HAD NATURAL GRACE AND TALENT, BUT THAT HER BODY SHAPE WASN'T QUITE RIGHT FOR A PROFESSIONAL DANCER. IT'S NOT FAIR!

MISS ELISE ASKED ME TO COME TRAIN WITH YOU. SHE ALSO INVITED TWO GRADE SIX GIRLS...

SOMEONE TOLD ME SHE HAD A FRIEND COMING TO OBSERVE, AND SHE WANTS TO IMPRESS HER!

OH! I WISH SHE'D TOLD US! I COULD HAVE PREPARED A LITTLE MORE.

FIFTEEN MINUTES LATER...

THIS IS MY VERY DEAR FRIEND *SYLVIE*. SHE'S A DANCE TEACHER TOO, AND I'VE WANTED HER TO WATCH ONE OF OUR CLASSES.

I KNOW YOU WILL DANCE YOUR VERY BEST FOR HER!

SUSHILA, STRETCH THAT LEG... PUSH YOURSELF! JODIE, EXCELLENT, KEEP GOING!

THE MUSIC... THE DANCE...THIS IS SO NICE...

AFTERWARDS...

AND WHY THE THREE OF US?

DO YOU THINK WE'RE GOING TO GET CHEWED OUT? BUT WE DANCED WELL--

COME IN!

WHY DID MISS ELISE ASK US TO GO BY HER OFFICE?

SUSHILA, JODIE, SUMMER... I'D LIKE YOU TO MEET SYLVIE RICHELLE!

SYLVIE ROCHELLE? THAT REMINDS ME OF SOMETHING! OH, YEAH, SHE DANCED WITH THE ROYAL BALLET IN THE 1970S!

SHE WAS MOST IMPRESSED WITH YOU ALL IN CLASS TODAY. WELL DONE!

THANK YOU, MISS ELISE! THANK YOU, MISS...UM... ROCHELLE.

AFTER DANCING FOR YEARS, I'VE DEVOTED MYSELF TO TEACHING. I'VE BEEN GIVING CLASSES IN FRANCE AND THEN AT THE ROYAL BALLET SCHOOL.

I HAVE A PICTURE OF YOU IN THE FIREBIRD!

AH, YES. A LONG TIME AGO, THAT WAS!

FOR A YEAR OR SO NOW, SYLVIE HAS BEEN WORKING ON A PROJECT OF HER OWN.

AN INDEPENDENT DANCE SCHOOL FOR BOARDERS IN THE SOUTH OF ENGLAND: THE ROCHELLE ACADEMY.

A LITTLE LIKE THE ROYAL BALLET, BUT MORE MODERN!

WE ARE AUDITIONING FOR THE LAST FEW SCHOLARSHIP PLACES AT ROCHELLE ACADEMY THIS AUGUST. I WOULD LIKE IT VERY MUCH IF YOU THREE GIRLS WOULD TRY OUT.

YOU MUST WORK HARD AND PUT DANCE ABOVE EVERYTHING ELSE!

NO WAY!

WE'RE READY. WE'LL MAKE IT, I PROMISE YOU.

WOW!

WHAT IS IT? WHAT HAPPENED? SOMETHING DID, I KNOW! SOMETHING GOOD?

YOU'VE MANAGED TO READ MY THOUGHTS. WE'RE NOT TWINS FOR NOTHING!

SOMETHING TO DO WITH THE FILM CREW AND THE MOVIE THEY'RE MAKING HERE THIS SUMMER?

NOTHING TO DO WITH THE FILM!

SOMETHING TO DO WITH DANCING THEN? TELL ME, SUMMER, PLEASE!

I'VE BEEN ASKED TO AUDITION TO ENTER THE ROCHELLE ACADEMY, A NEW DANCE SCHOOL. I WAS PICKED, AND JODIE, AND A SENIOR GIRL CALLED SUSHILA. CAN YOU BELIEVE IT?

OF COURSE, YOU'RE BRILLIANT, YOU KNOW!

MY SUPER-TALENTED SISTER!

IT'S JUST AN AUDITION, NOT AN ACTUAL PLACEMENT. I'LL HAVE TO WORK LIKE CRAZY IF I'M GOING TO STAND ANY KIND OF CHANCE!

YOU DIDN'T LAST TIME. YOU ALWAYS FAIL TESTS!

OH, NO... THE LITTLE VOICE IS BACK.

THREE DAYS LATER, AFTER SCHOOL...

SUMMER, I GOT THE BROCHURE FOR ROCHELLE ACADEMY, ALONG WITH A LETTER FROM MISS ELISE. THIS SCHOOL LOOKS TERRIFIC!

YES, BUT I MAY NOT BE SELECTED. I HAVE TO ACE THE AUDITION!

DADDY AND I WILL SUPPORT YOU IN ANY WAY WE CAN. YOU HAVE A TALENT, WE'VE ALWAYS KNOWN THAT. OF COURSE YOU MUST GO!

YOU WILL. I KNOW YOU WILL!

14

I'M SO JEALOUS! BOARDING SCHOOL! LIKE HOGWARTS! HOW COOL!

YOU CAN EVEN APPLY FOR A SCHOLARSHIP. HERE'S THE FORM...

IT'S COOL, BUT IT'LL BE MORE LIKE LEOTARDS AND LEG WARMERS THAN MAGIC WANDS AND INVISIBILITY CLOAKS!

THERE'S JUST ONE SNAG...

ACCORDING TO THE LETTER, YOUR AUDITION'S IN THE MIDDLE OF AUGUST, WHILE PADDY AND I ARE AWAY ON OUR HONEYMOON.

I'D HAVE LIKED TO BE THERE WITH YOU, LOOK AROUND, TALK TO THIS SYLVIE ROCHELLE!

OH...YOU'LL STILL BE AWAY?

YOUR AUDITION'S ON THAT SATURDAY MORNING, AND WE GET HOME THE FOLLOWING DAY.

MUM, IT'S NOT A PROBLEM. THERE'LL BE TIME TO LOOK AROUND IF I ACTUALLY EARN A SPOT. MISS ELISE CAN TAKE ME WITH JODIE AND SUSHILA TO THE AUDITION.

I KNOW, BUT ARE YOU SURE YOU'LL BE OKAY ON YOUR OWN?

SHE DOESN'T SAY IT OUT LOUD, BUT I KNOW WHAT SHE'S THINKING: "YOU ALREADY FAILED YOUR AUDITION TWO YEARS AGO." DAD WAS LATE, I ARRIVED SWEATING AND FLUSTERED AND LET THE CHANCE SLIP THROUGH MY FINGERS.

I WANTED DAD TO SEE ME DANCE, TO BE PROUD OF ME, TO LOVE ME SO MUCH HE'D CHANGE HIS MIND ABOUT THE DIVORCE. IT DIDN'T WORK OUT THAT WAY.

YOU'RE KIDDING ME, RIGHT? BOARDING SCHOOL?

DON'T YOU GET IT? THIS IS IMPORTANT. OPPORTUNITIES LIKE THIS COME JUST ONCE OR TWICE IN A LIFETIME, MAYBE!

NO, I REALLY DON'T GET IT!

SO YOU'RE INTO DANCE. WHY CAN'T YOU WAIT AND DO A DANCE CLASS AT THE UNIVERSITY OR SOMETHING?

THIS SHOULD BE A ROMANTIC MOMENT... HE COULD AT LEAST BE HAPPY FOR ME! HE'S ANNOYING ME!

IT DOESN'T WORK LIKE THAT.

NOT IF YOU WANT TO GET TO THE VERY TOP. YOU HAVE TO START YOUNG, GET THE BEST TEACHERS, REALLY PUSH YOURSELF!

GETTING PICKED IS A BIG DEAL, AARON. IF I GET THROUGH THE AUDITION, I'M GOING!

YOU SPEND ALL YOUR SPARE TIME ON BALLET AS IT IS!

WHAT ABOUT US?

IF I'M ACCEPTED TO THAT SCHOOL, I KNOW I'LL LOSE HIM. THERE ARE TONS OF GIRLS JUST WAITING.

AARON'S ARMS FEEL LIKE A PRISON...

DO YOU THINK WE HAVE A CHANCE?

YOU KNOW MISS ELISE IS ASKING US TO SIGN UP FOR PRIVATE LESSONS TO PREPARE US! NO CHARGE!

THAT'S GOOD!

I WANT ALL THREE OF YOU TO BE PREPARED FOR THIS. THEY'LL WANT TO SEE SOME BAR EXERCISES, A SET PIECE...I CAN HELP YOU PREPARE FOR THAT.

AND AN EXPRESSIVE DANCE TOO!

OKAY, CLASS IS STARTING!

AFTERWARDS...

TIME FOR A SMOOTHIE? BEFORE YOU CATCH YOUR BUS?

SURE!

YOU KNOW, IT WAS HORRIBLE AT MY LAST AUDITION TWO YEARS AGO. WHEN THEY TOLD ME I WAS TALENTED, BUT THAT I DIDN'T HAVE A DANCER'S BODY!

YOU HAVE TO HAVE A THICK SKIN IN THIS BUSINESS. YOU HAVE TO KEEP TRYING!

WHEN YOU WANT TO BECOME A DANCER, YOU WATCH YOUR FIGURE. YOU DON'T EAT THESE SORTS OF THINGS.

THAT LITTLE VOICE AGAIN!

YOU'RE NOT EATING YOUR CARROT CAKE?

I'M NOT VERY HUNGRY...

A FEW DAYS LATER...

THEY'RE HERE! THE FILM CREW IS HERE! COME ON, SUMMER, LET'S GO SEE!

I'M PRACTICING!

SO WHAT? YOU CAN DO THAT ANY TIME...IT'S NOT EVERY DAY A FILM CREW COMES TO THE VILLAGE!

IT'S LIKE A FESTIVAL! WE'LL GET TO SEE IT ALL.

YES, ESPECIALLY SINCE SOME OF THE PRODUCTION TEAM WILL STAY HERE IN THE B&B!

HOW WILL I CONCENTRATE WITH ALL THESE PEOPLE?

BY THE WAY, AREN'T YOU A LITTLE KEEN ON THE PRODUCER'S SON? WHAT WAS HIS NAME AGAIN?

JAMIE FINCH. DO YOU THINK HE MIGHT LIKE ME?

YOU KNOW THESE THINGS. YOU'VE GOT AARON...

JAMIE FINCH LIKES YOU. HE'LL BE LIVING HERE WITH THE PRODUCTION CREW.

YOUR EYES WILL MEET OVER THE BREAKFAST TABLE, WHILE COCO PLAYS THE VIOLIN—

YOU CAN'T KEEP FROM RUINING THAT MARVELOUS SCENE. COCO PLAYS LIKE A RUSTY PAN! HEE HEE!

STOP!

HEE HEE HEE!

HEE HEE HEE!

≥SHHH!≤ THEY'LL THINK WE'RE BONKERS!

18

YOU PREFER YOGURT TO THIS DELICIOUS CAKE WITH CARAMEL ICING?

IT WOULD BE A MISTAKE TO EAT THAT...

GET LOST, ALFIE. DANCERS DON'T EAT THAT KIND OF JUNK!

YOU COULD EAT ANYTHING YOU WANTED TO. YOU'RE REALLY SLIM AND PRETTY. AND DANCING MUST BURN UP A MILLION CALORIES A SECOND!

I'VE BEEN WATCHING YOU. YOU'VE BEEN SURVIVING ON RABBIT FOOD LATELY!

ARE YOU SPYING ON ME NOW?

WHAT'S UP? IS HE BUGGING YOU, SUMMER?

NO MORE THAN USUAL. HE'S TRYING TO GET ME TO EAT THAT DISGUSTING CAKE!

SHE'S KEEPING AN EYE ON HER FIGURE. AND SO AM I. GO AWAY!

IT IS TEMPTING, BUT NO, IT'S A BAD IDEA!

SHE TOLD YOU SHE DIDN'T WANT YOUR CAKE!

AARON ANNOYS ME MORE EVERY TIME I SEE HIM!

WHERE DOES HE GET OFF WATCHING MY FIGURE? THAT'S MY BUSINESS!

WE'LL BE ON VACATION SOON. WHAT IF WE THREW A PARTY AT TANGLEWOOD?

YEAH, THAT'D BE COOL! WE'LL INVITE SOME BOYS!

ALFIE, FOR INSTANCE!

NO OFFENSE, *MILLIE*, I KNOW YOU LIKE ALFIE. HE ISN'T BAD-LOOKING, BUT HE'S JUST SUCH A CLOWN!

YOU'RE JUDGMENTAL. ALFIE'S NICE!

SHE'S RIGHT. ALFIE EVEN GOT THE "MATH WHIZ" PRIZE AT THE HONORS CEREMONY YESTERDAY.

AND I GOT "MOST ORIGINAL STYLE," I'M PROUD TO SAY!

AND YOU GOT "MOST LIKELY TO SUCCEED," SUMMER... AWESOME!

I HOPE IT WILL BRING ME LUCK FOR MY AUDITION!

YOU AND AARON MAKE A REALLY GREAT COUPLE!

I WOULDN'T KNOW...

WEEEEEEEEEE!

OH, NO, NOT HIM!

GROSS! PULL YOUR TROUSERS UP, ALFIE!

I TOLD YOU ALFIE AND HIS FRIENDS ARE DIMWITS!

SKYE, DO YOU THINK THEY'D ACTUALLY LET US WATCH THE FILMING? MAYBE THEY NEED SOME EXTRAS?

IF ANYONE WAS GOING TO GET A BIT PART, IT WOULD BE SUMMER. SHE'D BE BRILLIANT!

I MIGHT GET NOTICED AND START A CAREER AS AN ACTRESS...

GO AWAY!

BE GOOD FOR GRANDMA KATE. YOUR CURFEW IS ELEVEN, SO NO LATER THAN THAT, PROMISE?

ELEVEN? SERIOUSLY? I'M FIFTEEN, NOT FIVE!

ELEVEN. THE LAST THING I WANT IS GRANDMA KATE WORRYING ABOUT WHERE YOU ARE. OKAY?

OKAY, OKAY!

HARRY WILL KEEP THE CHOCOLATE SHOP TICKING ALONG NICELY BUT, IF THERE ARE ANY PROBLEMS...

IT'S ALL UNDER CONTROL. THE GIRLS WILL HELP ME WITH THE B&B. WE'LL MANAGE JUST FINE!

BUT THREE WEEKS...I DON'T KNOW. SOMETHING COULD GO WRONG...

NO WAY! DON'T WORRY!

I SO WISH I COULD BE HERE FOR YOUR AUDITION. I'LL BE THINKING OF YOU!

DON'T CRY... DON'T CRY...

BON VOYAGE!

WHO WANTS FRENCH TOAST?

ME! ME!

NOT ME, I'M NOT HUNGRY. I'M GOING TO PRACTICE!

EVEN IF MY STOMACH'S GROWLING WITH HUNGER, I'M GETTING USED TO THE EMPTY FEELING. IT MAKES ME FEEL LIGHT, CLEAN, STRONG.

THE NEXT DAY...

I CAN'T DO IT! I FEEL HEAVY, NUMB...

HELLO, SUMMER. YOU'RE EARLY. I THOUGHT I'D BE THE FIRST HERE TODAY!

IF SHE KNEW I'D BEEN HERE TWO HOURS ALREADY, SHE'D THINK I WAS DESPERATE FOR THE AUDITION!

WOULDN'T IT BE AMAZING IF WE WERE SELECTED? COME SEPTEMBER, WE'D BE AT BALLET SCHOOL FULL-TIME. I CAN'T STOP THINKING ABOUT IT. I'M GOING TO PRACTICE EVERY DAY UNTIL THE AUDITION!

ME, TOO. I'D DO ANYTHING TO GET A PLACE, ANYTHING AT ALL.

THAT AFTERNOON...

UH...HELLO. I'M JAMIE FINCH, THE SON OF *NIKKI* THE PRODUCER!

WELCOME TO THE MADHOUSE, JAMIE!

THANK YOU FOR HAVING ME. I'M SO EXCITED TO BE OUT OF LONDON FOR A WHILE! BY THE WAY, JUST CALL ME FINCH, EVERYONE ELSE DOES!

HEY, SKYE!

UH...UM... HELLO!

UH HUH...FINCH JUST CAUSED A REAL TIDAL WAVE IN MY SISTER'S HEART!

I'M HAPPY FOR HER, BUT I HAVE A FEELING THAT MY LIFE WILL NEVER BE THE SAME AGAIN. SKYE'S GOING TO PULL AWAY FROM ME!

EARLY MONDAY AFTERNOON...

THE FILM CREW'S LOOKING FOR EXTRAS!

WE COULD BE FAMOUS!

GET A GRIP. ROBERT PATTINSON ISN'T IN THIS FILM!

THE COSTUMER OFFERED TO LET ME GIVE HER A HAND WITH COSTUMES, SO I CAN MAKE SURE YOU GET A COOL HAT OR A PARASOL AT THE EXTRAS MEETING. FINCH SAYS IT SHOULD BE A LOT OF FUN!

OH, WELL, IF FINCH SAYS SO!

WHERE ARE YOU GOING? YOU DON'T HAVE BALLET LESSONS TODAY!

NO, BUT I WANT TO USE THE STUDIO TO PRACTICE!

BUT...WE'RE GOING TO THE BEACH! I TOLD AARON! HE'S COMING AFTER HIS SOCCER MATCH!

WHY DID SHE INVITE AARON? WHAT BUSINESS IS IT OF HERS?

I'M BUSY. TOO BUSY FOR SWIMMING AND SUNBATHING. SORRY, GIRLS, I'LL JOIN YOU LATER!

MY STOMACH IS CHURNING. FOOD, LIKE FUN, HAS BEEN SIDELINED.

FINALLY! I THOUGHT YOU'D NEVER GET HERE!

WELL, HERE I AM!

DON'T, AARON. PEOPLE ARE LOOKING!

YOU'RE NO FUN. YOU'RE SO...UPTIGHT LATELY. ALL YOU THINK ABOUT IS BALLET AND THAT STUPID AUDITION!

I'LL GO SEE THE OTHERS!

YOU OKAY? YOU LOOK FED UP.

I'M JUST... TIRED.

AH, YES. YOU'RE PRACTICING A LOT LATELY. WE'RE ALL ROOTING FOR YOU, Y'KNOW! YOU'RE GOING TO ACE IT! I BET THAT YOU'D DO IT!

YOU HAVE A BET?

I'M SURE THIS THING ABOUT A BET IS BECAUSE OF AARON. AND HE BET I'D FAIL THE AUDITION. AM I RIGHT?

WELL, UH, HE JUST SAYS STUFF, TO BE FUNNY!

ME AND MY BIG MOUTH. I'VE PUT MY FOOT IN IT MASSIVELY!

IT'S NOT YOUR FAULT MY BOYFRIEND'S A CREEP.

HEY, SUMMER, COME ON. LET'S HAVE FUN WITH THE OTHERS. DO YOU WANT A MARSHMALLOW?

NO!

YOU'RE GETTING THIN! THERE'S NOTHING FOR ME TO HOLD ON TO!

SO DON'T THEN. DON'T BOTHER.

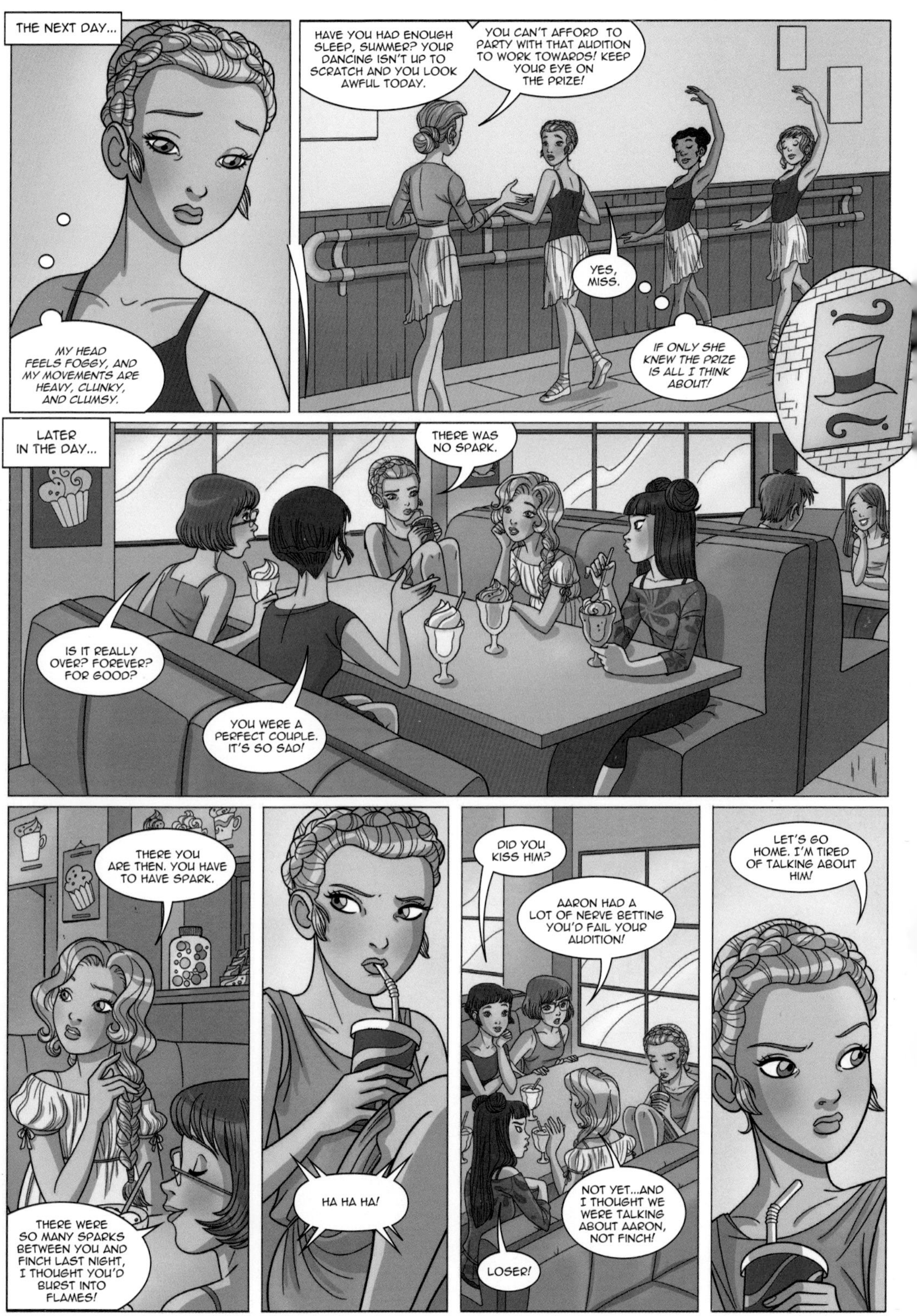
THE NEXT DAY...
MY HEAD FEELS FOGGY, AND MY MOVEMENTS ARE HEAVY, CLUNKY, AND CLUMSY.
HAVE YOU HAD ENOUGH SLEEP, SUMMER? YOUR DANCING ISN'T UP TO SCRATCH AND YOU LOOK AWFUL TODAY.
YOU CAN'T AFFORD TO PARTY WITH THAT AUDITION TO WORK TOWARDS! KEEP YOUR EYE ON THE PRIZE!
YES, MISS.
IF ONLY SHE KNEW THE PRIZE IS ALL I THINK ABOUT!
LATER IN THE DAY...
THERE WAS NO SPARK.
IS IT REALLY OVER? FOREVER? FOR GOOD?
YOU WERE A PERFECT COUPLE. IT'S SO SAD!
THERE YOU ARE THEN. YOU HAVE TO HAVE SPARK.
THERE WERE SO MANY SPARKS BETWEEN YOU AND FINCH LAST NIGHT, I THOUGHT YOU'D BURST INTO FLAMES!
HA HA HA!
DID YOU KISS HIM?
AARON HAD A LOT OF NERVE BETTING YOU'D FAIL YOUR AUDITION!
NOT YET...AND I THOUGHT WE WERE TALKING ABOUT AARON, NOT FINCH!
LOSER!
LET'S GO HOME. I'M TIRED OF TALKING ABOUT HIM!

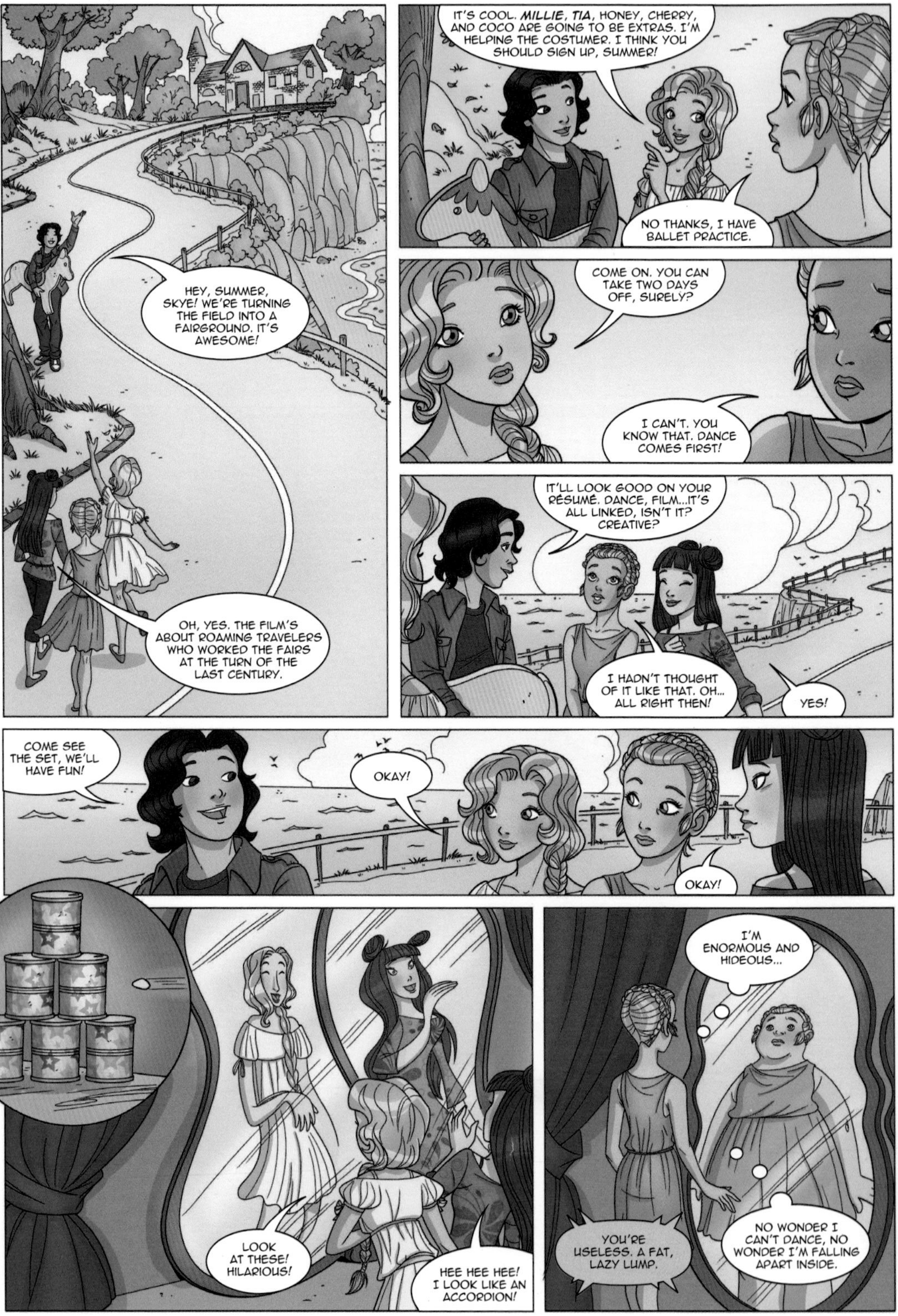
HEY, SUMMER, SKYE! WE'RE TURNING THE FIELD INTO A FAIRGROUND. IT'S AWESOME!
OH, YES. THE FILM'S ABOUT ROAMING TRAVELERS WHO WORKED THE FAIRS AT THE TURN OF THE LAST CENTURY.
IT'S COOL. MILLIE, TIA, HONEY, CHERRY, AND COCO ARE GOING TO BE EXTRAS. I'M HELPING THE COSTUMER. I THINK YOU SHOULD SIGN UP, SUMMER!
NO THANKS, I HAVE BALLET PRACTICE.
COME ON. YOU CAN TAKE TWO DAYS OFF, SURELY?
I CAN'T. YOU KNOW THAT. DANCE COMES FIRST!
IT'LL LOOK GOOD ON YOUR RÉSUMÉ. DANCE, FILM...IT'S ALL LINKED, ISN'T IT? CREATIVE?
I HADN'T THOUGHT OF IT LIKE THAT. OH... ALL RIGHT THEN!
YES!
COME SEE THE SET, WE'LL HAVE FUN!
OKAY!
OKAY!
LOOK AT THESE! HILARIOUS!
HEE HEE HEE! I LOOK LIKE AN ACCORDION!
I'M ENORMOUS AND HIDEOUS...
YOU'RE USELESS. A FAT, LAZY LUMP.
NO WONDER I CAN'T DANCE, NO WONDER I'M FALLING APART INSIDE.

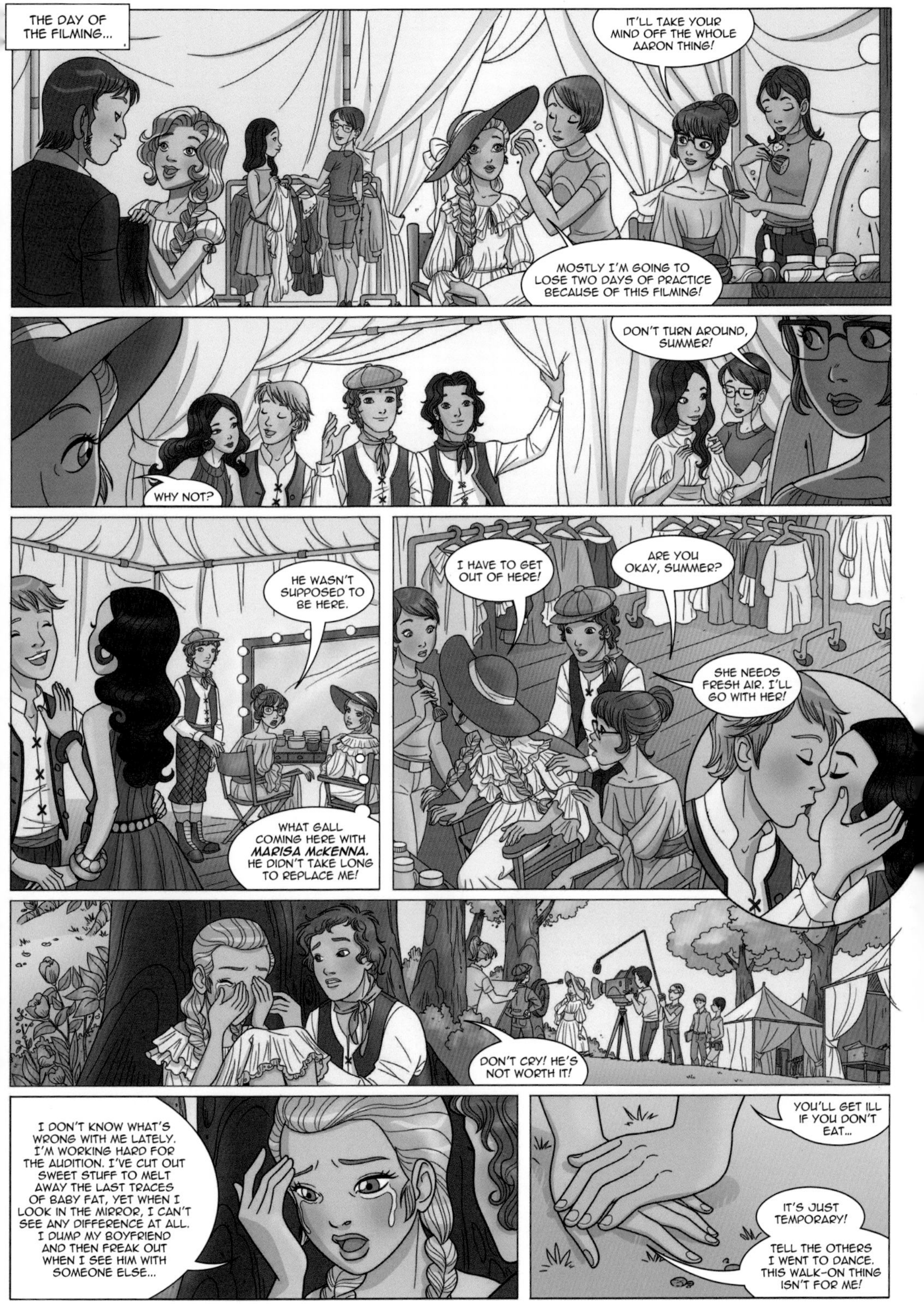
THE DAY OF THE FILMING...
IT'LL TAKE YOUR MIND OFF THE WHOLE AARON THING!
MOSTLY I'M GOING TO LOSE TWO DAYS OF PRACTICE BECAUSE OF THIS FILMING!
DON'T TURN AROUND, SUMMER!
WHY NOT?
HE WASN'T SUPPOSED TO BE HERE.
WHAT GALL COMING HERE WITH MARISA McKENNA. HE DIDN'T TAKE LONG TO REPLACE ME!
I HAVE TO GET OUT OF HERE!
ARE YOU OKAY, SUMMER?
SHE NEEDS FRESH AIR. I'LL GO WITH HER!
DON'T CRY! HE'S NOT WORTH IT!
I DON'T KNOW WHAT'S WRONG WITH ME LATELY. I'M WORKING HARD FOR THE AUDITION. I'VE CUT OUT SWEET STUFF TO MELT AWAY THE LAST TRACES OF BABY FAT, YET WHEN I LOOK IN THE MIRROR, I CAN'T SEE ANY DIFFERENCE AT ALL. I DUMP MY BOYFRIEND AND THEN FREAK OUT WHEN I SEE HIM WITH SOMEONE ELSE...
YOU'LL GET ILL IF YOU DON'T EAT...
IT'S JUST TEMPORARY!
TELL THE OTHERS I WENT TO DANCE. THIS WALK-ON THING ISN'T FOR ME!

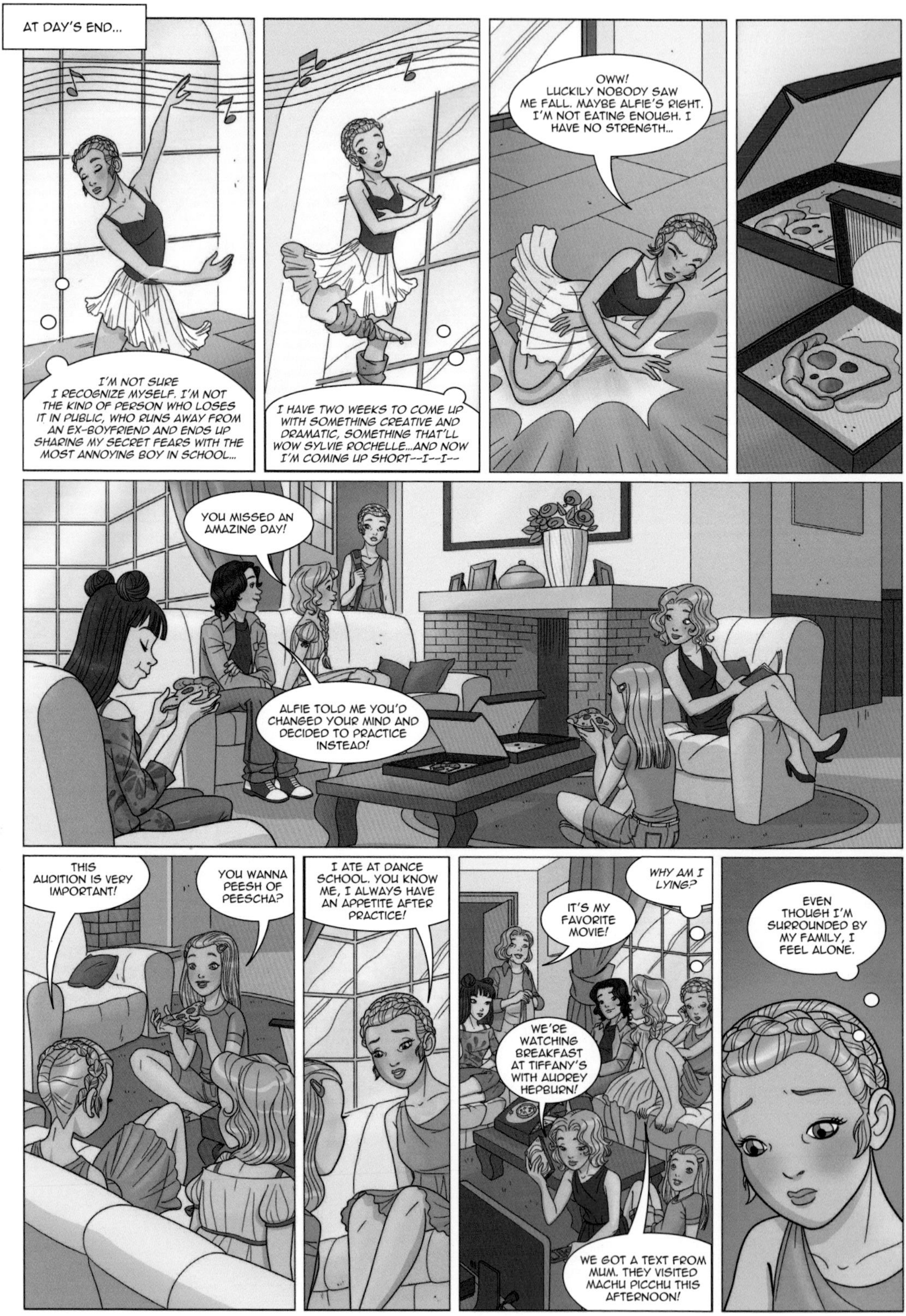

AT DAY'S END...
I'M NOT SURE I RECOGNIZE MYSELF. I'M NOT THE KIND OF PERSON WHO LOSES IT IN PUBLIC, WHO RUNS AWAY FROM AN EX-BOYFRIEND AND ENDS UP SHARING MY SECRET FEARS WITH THE MOST ANNOYING BOY IN SCHOOL...
I HAVE TWO WEEKS TO COME UP WITH SOMETHING CREATIVE AND DRAMATIC, SOMETHING THAT'LL WOW SYLVIE ROCHELLE...AND NOW I'M COMING UP SHORT--I--I--
OWW! LUCKILY NOBODY SAW ME FALL. MAYBE ALFIE'S RIGHT. I'M NOT EATING ENOUGH. I HAVE NO STRENGTH...
YOU MISSED AN AMAZING DAY!
ALFIE TOLD ME YOU'D CHANGED YOUR MIND AND DECIDED TO PRACTICE INSTEAD!
THIS AUDITION IS VERY IMPORTANT!
YOU WANNA PEESH OF PEESCHA?
I ATE AT DANCE SCHOOL. YOU KNOW ME, I ALWAYS HAVE AN APPETITE AFTER PRACTICE!
WHY AM I LYING?
IT'S MY FAVORITE MOVIE!
WE'RE WATCHING BREAKFAST AT TIFFANY'S WITH AUDREY HEPBURN!
WE GOT A TEXT FROM MUM. THEY VISITED MACHU PICCHU THIS AFTERNOON!
EVEN THOUGH I'M SURROUNDED BY MY FAMILY, I FEEL ALONE.

SUMMER, WHAT'S GOING ON? IT'S A STRONG PIECE OF MUSIC, BUT THE DANCE DOESN'T MATCH UP TO IT.

IT'S ROUGH, UNFORMED, AMATEURISH!

HAVEN'T YOU BEEN WORKING ON IT?

I HAVE, OF COURSE.

YOU'RE ONE OF THE BEST PUPILS I HAVE. YOU HAVE POTENTIAL. THESE LAST TWO WEEKS, YOU'VE BEEN TIRED, SLOW, LACKLUSTER. FIND THE SPARK, THE PASSION!

THAT ELUSIVE SPARK AGAIN THAT I DON'T HAVE, NOT WITH BOYS, NOT WITH DANCING... WHEN DID I LOSE IT?

MISS ELISE WAS TOTALLY PICKING ON YOU TODAY. EVERYONE HAS AN OFF DAY SOMETIMES!

YOUR MUM AND YOUR STEPDAD ARE AWAY, AND YOU'VE GOT ALL THOSE FILM PEOPLE STAYING IN THE HOUSE. YOU JUST BROKE UP WITH AARON--ALL THAT IS STRESSFUL!

I'M FINE, IT'S NOTHING TO DO WITH THAT!

ALL I WANT IT IS TO GET INTO THE ROCHELLE ACADEMY. I'LL DO ANYTHING TO MAKE IT THERE!

THE PROBLEM IS I COULD BE SLIMMER, LIGHTER, THEN I MIGHT STAND A BETTER CHANCE AT THE AUDITION.

THAT'S WHY YOU'RE STARVING YOURSELF?

WE'RE THIRTEEN... THAT'S WAY TOO YOUNG FOR CRASH DIETS! YOU'RE NOT FAT, SUMMER!

YOU NEED VITAMINS, MINERALS, AND PROTEIN OR YOU WON'T BE ABLE TO DANCE YOUR BEST!

LEAVE ME ALONE!

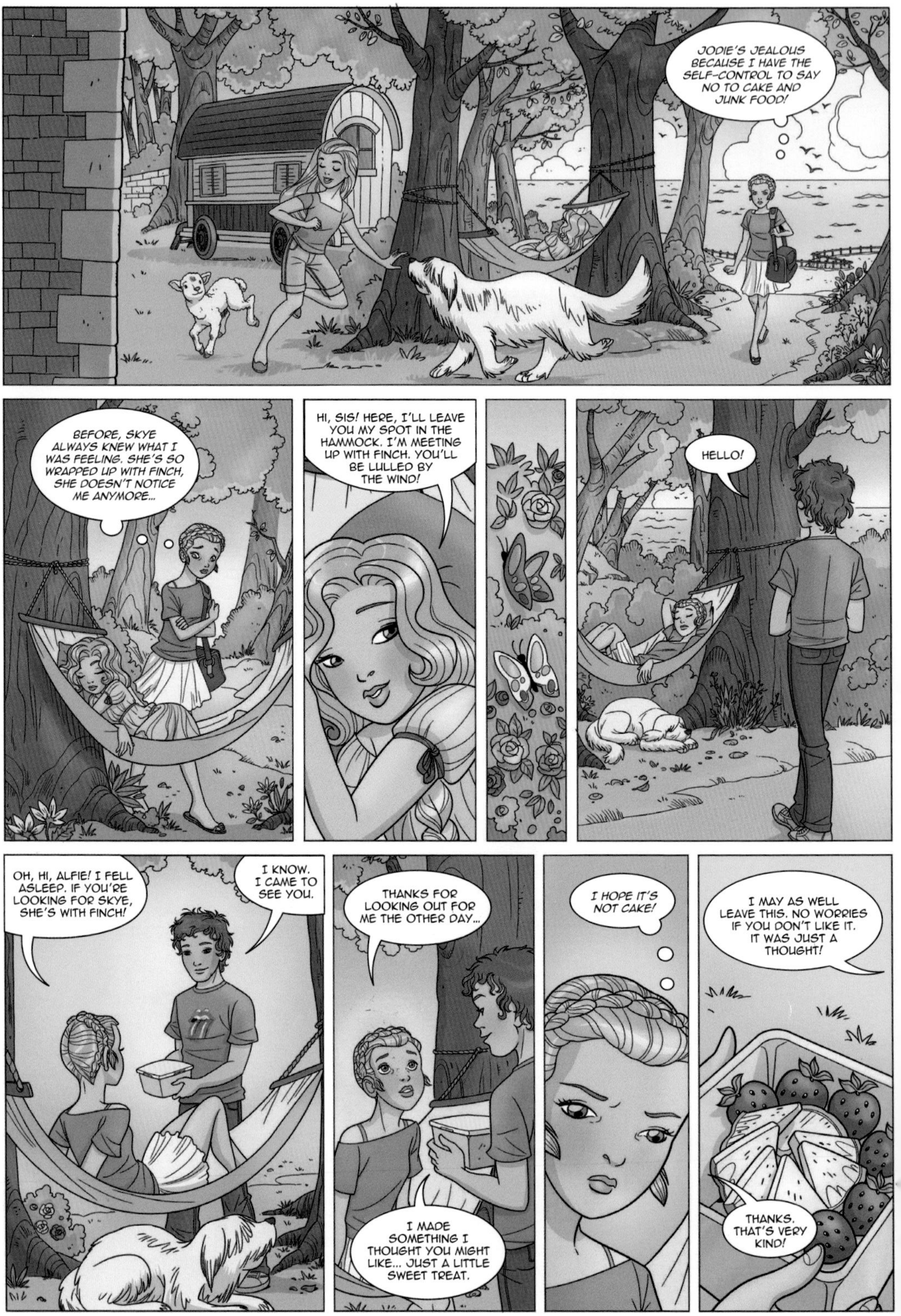
JODIE'S JEALOUS BECAUSE I HAVE THE SELF-CONTROL TO SAY NO TO CAKE AND JUNK FOOD!
BEFORE, SKYE ALWAYS KNEW WHAT I WAS FEELING. SHE'S SO WRAPPED UP WITH FINCH, SHE DOESN'T NOTICE ME ANYMORE...
HI, SIS! HERE, I'LL LEAVE YOU MY SPOT IN THE HAMMOCK. I'M MEETING UP WITH FINCH. YOU'LL BE LULLED BY THE WIND!
HELLO!
OH, HI, ALFIE! I FELL ASLEEP. IF YOU'RE LOOKING FOR SKYE, SHE'S WITH FINCH!
I KNOW. I CAME TO SEE YOU.
THANKS FOR LOOKING OUT FOR ME THE OTHER DAY...
I MADE SOMETHING I THOUGHT YOU MIGHT LIKE... JUST A LITTLE SWEET TREAT.
I HOPE IT'S NOT CAKE!
I MAY AS WELL LEAVE THIS. NO WORRIES IF YOU DON'T LIKE IT. IT WAS JUST A THOUGHT!
THANKS. THAT'S VERY KIND!

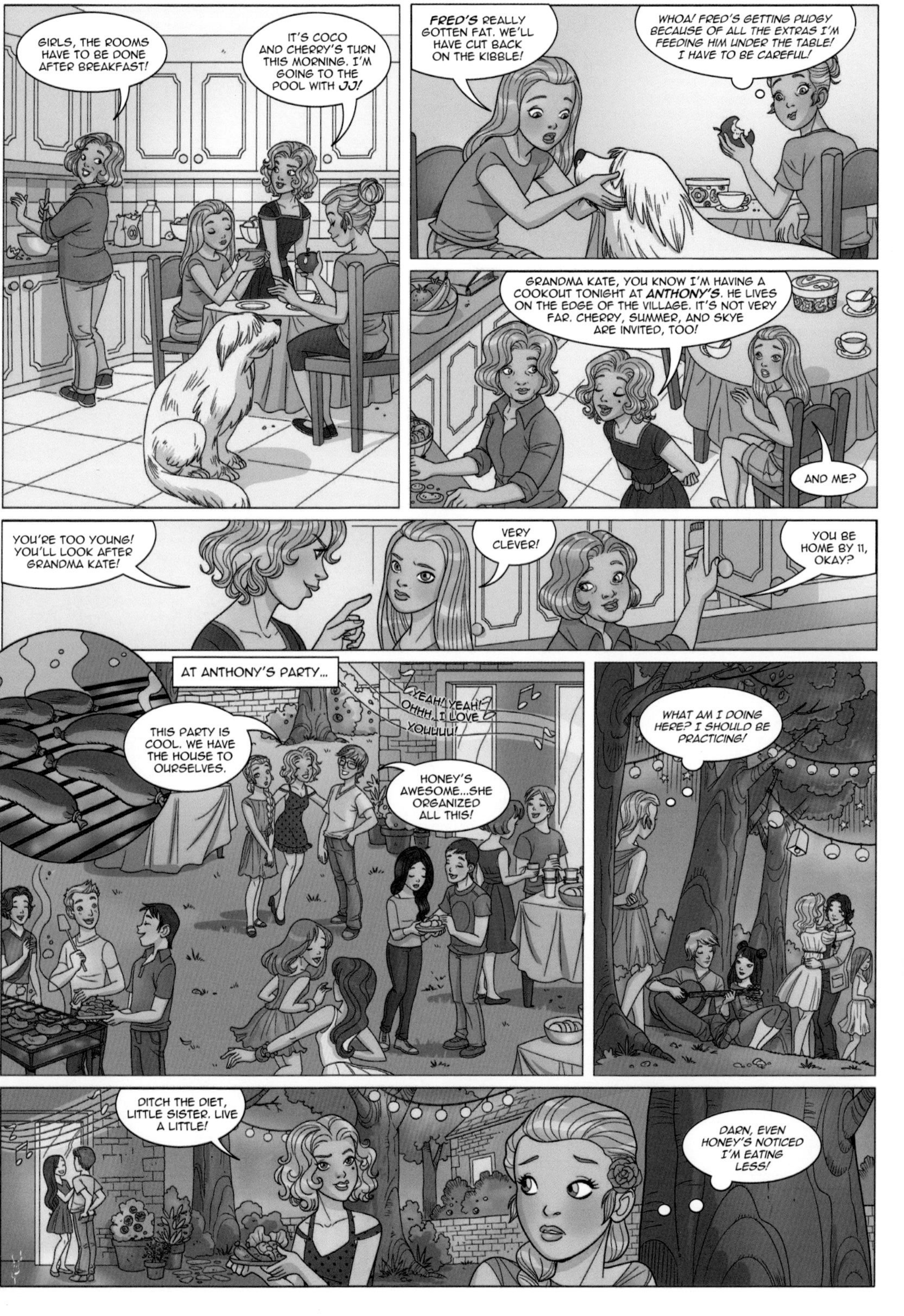
GIRLS, THE ROOMS HAVE TO BE DONE AFTER BREAKFAST!
IT'S COCO AND CHERRY'S TURN THIS MORNING. I'M GOING TO THE POOL WITH JJ!
FRED'S REALLY GOTTEN FAT. WE'LL HAVE CUT BACK ON THE KIBBLE!
WHOA! FRED'S GETTING PUDGY BECAUSE OF ALL THE EXTRAS I'M FEEDING HIM UNDER THE TABLE! I HAVE TO BE CAREFUL!
GRANDMA KATE, YOU KNOW I'M HAVING A COOKOUT TONIGHT AT ANTHONY'S. HE LIVES ON THE EDGE OF THE VILLAGE. IT'S NOT VERY FAR. CHERRY, SUMMER, AND SKYE ARE INVITED, TOO!
AND ME?
YOU'RE TOO YOUNG! YOU'LL LOOK AFTER GRANDMA KATE!
VERY CLEVER!
YOU BE HOME BY 11, OKAY?
AT ANTHONY'S PARTY...
YEAH! YEAH! OHHH, I LOVE YOUUUU!
THIS PARTY IS COOL. WE HAVE THE HOUSE TO OURSELVES.
HONEY'S AWESOME...SHE ORGANIZED ALL THIS!
WHAT AM I DOING HERE? I SHOULD BE PRACTICING!
DITCH THE DIET, LITTLE SISTER. LIVE A LITTLE!
DARN, EVEN HONEY'S NOTICED I'M EATING LESS!

YOU WANT SOME PUNCH, HONEY?

OH, YES, I DO!

SHE HAS HIM DANGLING ON A STRING LIKE A YO-YO. SHE REELS HIM IN WITH A FLUTTER OF HER LASHES; THE NEXT MINUTE SHE LETS HIM GO AGAIN.

IS SHE GOING OUT WITH JJ? BUT ANTHONY'S PRETTY SMITTEN, ISN'T HE?

THAT'S HONEY. SHE'S KIND OF HARD TO PIN DOWN.

IS THAT A TRAMPOLINE DOWN AT THE BOTTOM OF THE GARDEN?

WANT TO GO?

THIS IS SO FUN!

YEAH!

I LIKE YOUR FLOWER CLIP.

I LIKE THE FLOWER, TOO. IT WAS A CHRISTMAS PRESENT. AARON LEFT IT IN MY LOCKER WITH AN UNSIGNED CARD. ROMANTIC, RIGHT?

ONE DAY I'LL TELL HER I'M THE ONE WHO PUT IT IN HER LOCKER!

ANYHOW, I'M THROUGH WITH ROMANCE. I'M GOING TO CONCENTRATE ON MY CAREER INSTEAD. ARE YOU CRUSHING ON ANYONE?

ME? I--I'M INTERESTED IN A GIRL WHO DOESN'T KNOW. I'M WAITING FOR THE RIGHT MOMENT TO TELL HER I LOVE HER.

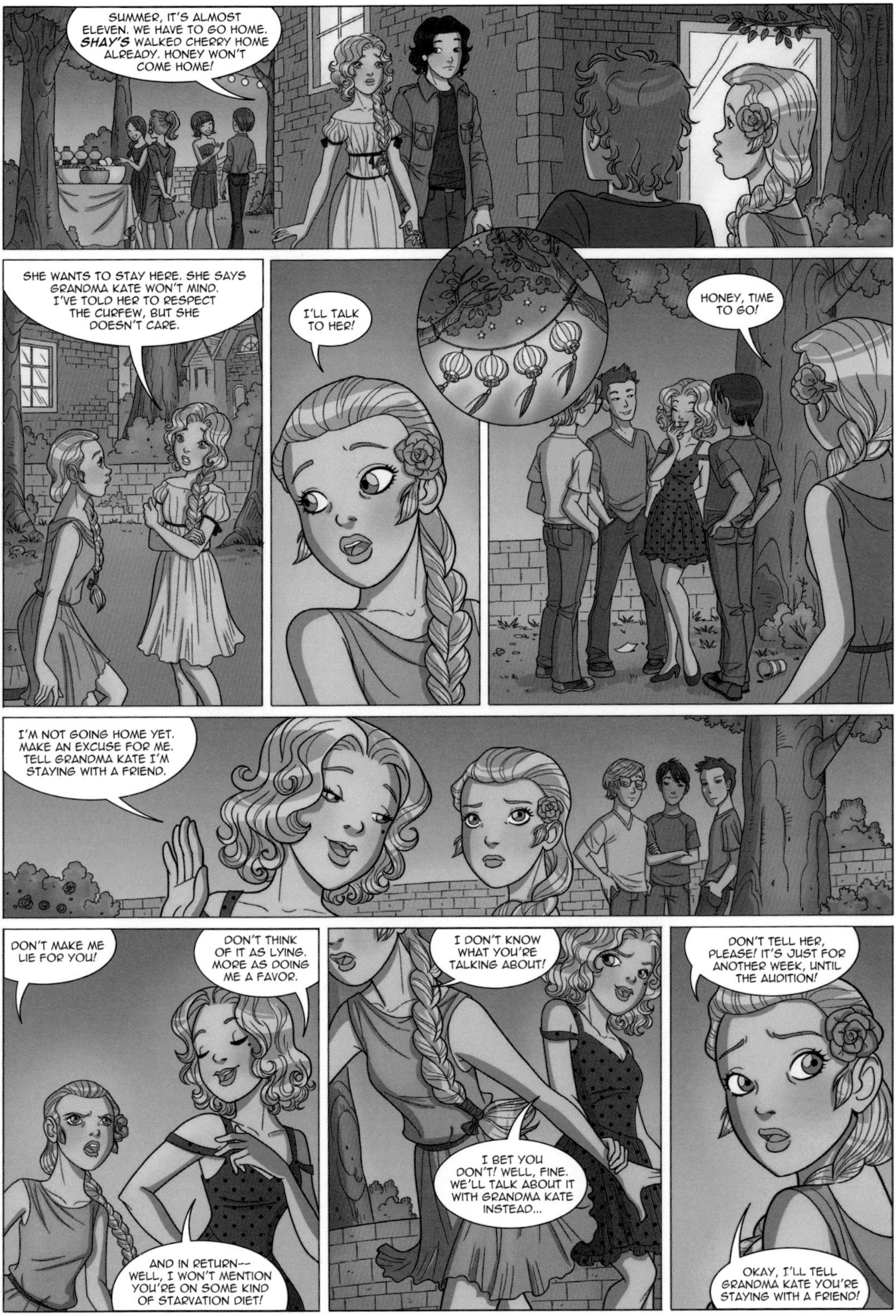
SUMMER, IT'S ALMOST ELEVEN. WE HAVE TO GO HOME. SHAY'S WALKED CHERRY HOME ALREADY. HONEY WON'T COME HOME!
SHE WANTS TO STAY HERE. SHE SAYS GRANDMA KATE WON'T MIND. I'VE TOLD HER TO RESPECT THE CURFEW, BUT SHE DOESN'T CARE.
I'LL TALK TO HER!
HONEY, TIME TO GO!
I'M NOT GOING HOME YET. MAKE AN EXCUSE FOR ME. TELL GRANDMA KATE I'M STAYING WITH A FRIEND.
DON'T MAKE ME LIE FOR YOU!
DON'T THINK OF IT AS LYING. MORE AS DOING ME A FAVOR.
AND IN RETURN-- WELL, I WON'T MENTION YOU'RE ON SOME KIND OF STARVATION DIET!
I DON'T KNOW WHAT YOU'RE TALKING ABOUT!
I BET YOU DON'T! WELL, FINE. WE'LL TALK ABOUT IT WITH GRANDMA KATE INSTEAD...
DON'T TELL HER, PLEASE! IT'S JUST FOR ANOTHER WEEK, UNTIL THE AUDITION!
OKAY, I'LL TELL GRANDMA KATE YOU'RE STAYING WITH A FRIEND!

BAKING MUFFINS IS LIKE TORTURE. MY STOMACH'S GROWLING AND MY MOUTH'S WATERING, BUT I WON'T WEAKEN!

FOR YOU, GRANDMA!

THANK YOU, HONEY! NEXT TIME, WHEN YOU STAY OVER WITH A FRIEND, LET ME KNOW AHEAD OF TIME. OKAY?

YOU MADE THEM, AREN'T YOU GOING TO EAT ONE?

OF COURSE!

I WANT TO SLAP HER.

WE HAD A DEAL, REMEMBER?

WITH MUM AWAY, HONEY IS OUT OF CONTROL AGAIN, AND THIS TIME, INSTEAD OF CHERRY OR PADDY, SHE'S GOT IT IN FOR ME!

JUST A LITTLE MORE. YOU CAN DO IT. I KNOW YOU CAN!

SUNDAY, AT DANCE SCHOOL...

IF SYLVIE ROCHELLE HAS TO CHOOSE BETWEEN A CURVY GIRL AND A SLIM ONE, SHE'D HAVE TO CHOOSE THE SLIM ONE...MEANING ME!

THE TROUBLE IS I HAVEN'T QUITE LOST ENOUGH. MY THIGHS ARE STILL TOO BIG!

JODIE KEEPS LOOKING AT ME. I'M NOT FOOLED. SHE CAN SEE I'VE LOST WEIGHT, AND IT'S A THREAT TO HER.

HURRY, SUSHILA. I'M WAITING FOR YOU!

I'M GOING ON. MEET ME IN THE STUDIO?

EXCUSE ME. I MISJUDGED THINGS A LITTLE LAST TIME. I SUGGESTED YOU WEREN'T TAKING THINGS SERIOUSLY...

I CAN SEE THAT YOU ARE. I'M WONDERING NOW IF PERHAPS YOU'RE PUSHING YOURSELF A LITTLE TOO HARD?

TOO HARD? SATURDAY'S AUDITION DAY!

SOME OF YOUR CLASSMATES SEEM TO BE WORRIED ABOUT YOU, AND NOW THAT I'M AWARE OF IT, I'M CONCERNED, TOO.

YOUR ENERGY LEVELS ARE VERY UP AND DOWN. HAVE YOU BEEN DIETING?

JEALOUS, SPITEFUL JODIE SNITCHED!

I'M EATING WELL. I'M BEING CAREFUL... MAKING HEALTHY CHOICES... THAT'S ALL!

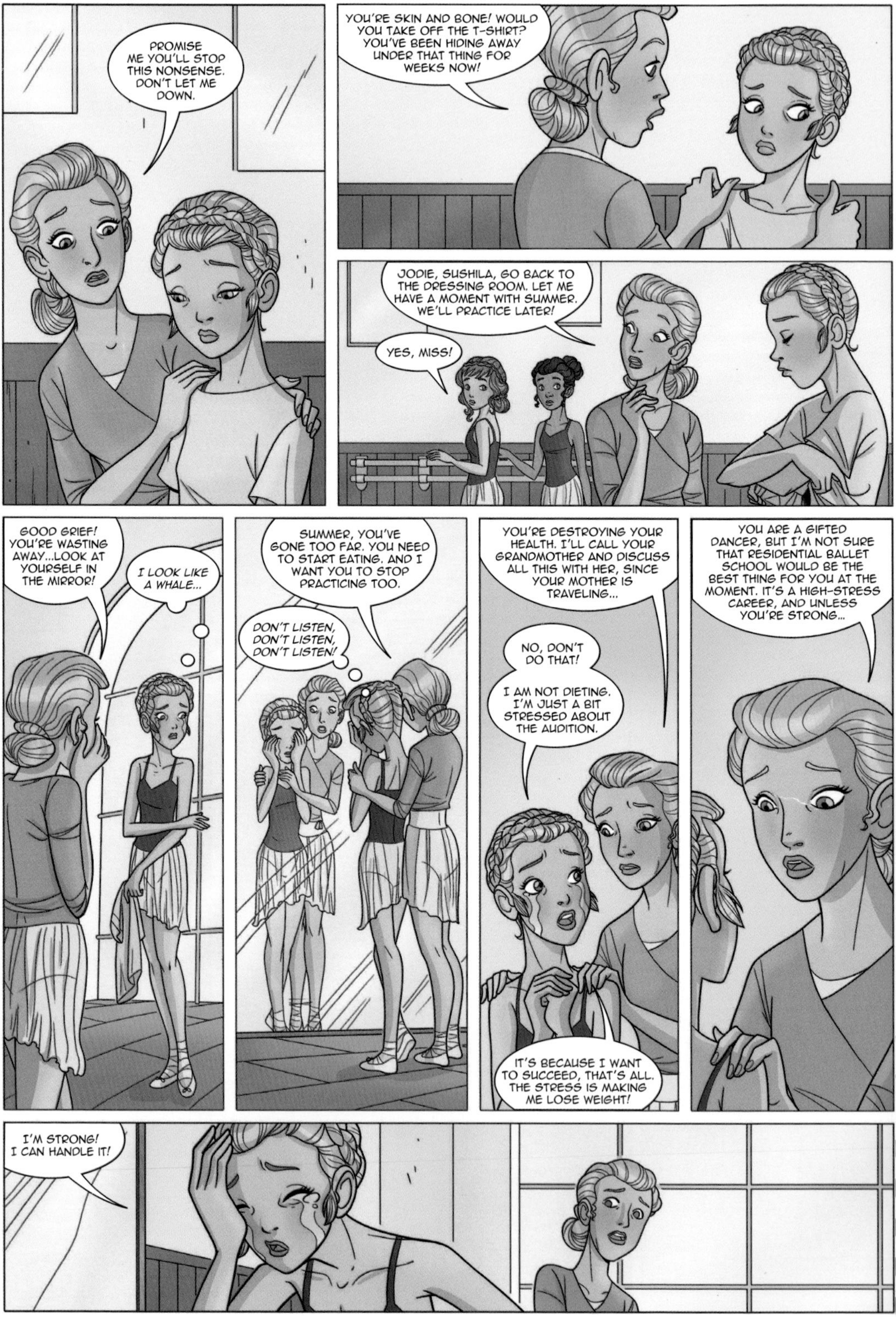
PROMISE ME YOU'LL STOP THIS NONSENSE. DON'T LET ME DOWN.
YOU'RE SKIN AND BONE! WOULD YOU TAKE OFF THE T-SHIRT? YOU'VE BEEN HIDING AWAY UNDER THAT THING FOR WEEKS NOW!
JODIE, SUSHILA, GO BACK TO THE DRESSING ROOM. LET ME HAVE A MOMENT WITH SUMMER. WE'LL PRACTICE LATER!
YES, MISS!
GOOD GRIEF! YOU'RE WASTING AWAY...LOOK AT YOURSELF IN THE MIRROR!
I LOOK LIKE A WHALE...
SUMMER, YOU'VE GONE TOO FAR. YOU NEED TO START EATING. AND I WANT YOU TO STOP PRACTICING TOO.
DON'T LISTEN, DON'T LISTEN, DON'T LISTEN!
YOU'RE DESTROYING YOUR HEALTH. I'LL CALL YOUR GRANDMOTHER AND DISCUSS ALL THIS WITH HER, SINCE YOUR MOTHER IS TRAVELING...
NO, DON'T DO THAT!
I AM NOT DIETING. I'M JUST A BIT STRESSED ABOUT THE AUDITION.
IT'S BECAUSE I WANT TO SUCCEED, THAT'S ALL. THE STRESS IS MAKING ME LOSE WEIGHT!
YOU ARE A GIFTED DANCER, BUT I'M NOT SURE THAT RESIDENTIAL BALLET SCHOOL WOULD BE THE BEST THING FOR YOU AT THE MOMENT. IT'S A HIGH-STRESS CAREER, AND UNLESS YOU'RE STRONG...
I'M STRONG! I CAN HANDLE IT!

I CAN'T TRUST MISS ELISE ANYMORE. AND JODIE'S NO LONGER MY FRIEND. IT'S ALL HER FAULT!

YOU'LL FAIL YOU HAVEN'T WORKED HARD ENOUGH. YOU'RE NOT GOOD ENOUGH!

ALFIE? WHAT'RE YOU DOING HERE?

I CAME BY TO WISH YOU GOOD LUCK FOR SATURDAY. AND YOU WEREN'T HOME, SO I THOUGHT I'D DO SOME SUNBATHING...

SUMMER...I'M VERY WORRIED ABOUT YOU. THIS DIET THING...

TALK TO SOMEBODY. YOUR MUM, YOUR GRAN, YOUR DAD, A DOCTOR. IT'S GETTING OUT OF HAND, AND I DON'T KNOW WHAT TO DO.

I'M SPEAKING TO YOU AS A FRIEND!

I KNOW. YOU'RE A TRUE FRIEND, ALFIE!

THAT'S MORE THAN I CAN SAY FOR TIA OR MILLIE LATELY, OR EVEN SKYE...I'VE PUSHED THEM ALL AWAY, MADE MYSELF TOO BUSY WITH PRACTICE, AND THEY LET IT HAPPEN. ALFIE'S THE ONLY ONE WHO'S REFUSED TO BE DISCOURAGED!

IT STOPS ONCE THE AUDITION IS OVER, YEAH?

DEFINITELY!

I THINK SO ANYWAY. I DON'T KNOW, I JUST CAN'T SEEM TO HELP IT!

THAT NIGHT...

HEY! YOU COULD KNOCK BEFORE COMING IN!

SUMMER! WHAT'S GOING ON? YOU'RE LIKE A SKELETON!

DON'T BE RIDICULOUS! I'M NO DIFFERENT! JUST A BIT MORE...TONED MAYBE. FROM ALL THE EXTRA DANCING!

I CAN SEE YOUR RIBS!

YOUR SHOULDER BLADES LOOKS LIKE THEY'D SLICE THROUGH YOUR SKIN!

I KNOW YOU'RE WATCHING WHAT YOU EAT, BUT...THIS IS SCARY, SUMMER! I HAD NO IDEA!

BECAUSE YOU'VE BEEN SO WRAPPED UP WITH FINCH. TOO BUSY FALLING IN LOVE TO NOTICE HOW LOST, HOW FRIGHTENED I AM!

SUMMER, STOP IT!

BACK OFF. I'M FINE!

38

HELLO...DAD? IT'S SUMMER!

ARE YOU ALL RIGHT?

YES, DAD. JUST FINE! IT'S TWO IN THE MORNING AND I'M SCARED BECAUSE MY LIFE'S FALLING TO BITS, BUT I'M JUST FINE...

I JUST WANTED TO TALK.

WELL...THAT'S VERY NICE, SUMMER, BUT I'M PRETTY BUSY RIGHT NOW. WAS THERE SOMETHING IN PARTICULAR?

NO, NO...I JUST WANTED TO TELL YOU I HAVE MY AUDITION ON SATURDAY. FOR THE DANCE SCHOOL. AND I'M A BIT...UM... NERVOUS.

SO YOU'RE IN A NEW DANCE SHOW, IS THAT IT?

DON'T WORRY, YOU'LL BE BRILLIANT AS USUAL. MY LITTLE BALLERINA. SORRY, IT'S CRAZY AT THE OFFICE TODAY. I HAVE TO GO, KISSES!

KISSES... THAT'S IT?

THE DAY OF THE AUDITION AT THE ROCHELLE ACADEMY...

A MESSAGE FROM MUM TELLING ME SHE LOVES ME, A MESSAGE FROM SKYE TELLING ME TO KNOCK THEIR SOCKS OFF, AND ONE FROM ALFIE WISHING ME LUCK AGAIN...

THIS IS IT. IT'S THE BIG DAY. I'M IN THE CHANGING ROOMS OF STUDIO ONE AT THE ROCHELLE ACADEMY... AND I'M SUPER NERVOUS!

OKAY?

NOT OKAY...

CANDY MAXWELL? YOU HAVE TEN MINUTES TO PRESENT YOUR PIECES.

YES, MA'AM!

TEN MINUTES...IS THAT ALL WE GET? AFTER EIGHT WEEKS OF STRESS AND ENDLESS PRACTICE!

YEAH... IT'S CRAZY!

IT'S JUST AN AUDITION. WE'VE PRACTICED, WE KNOW WHAT TO DO!

WHY ARE YOU BEING NICE TO ME? WHEN YOU SAID THINGS TO MISS ELISE ABOUT ME?

IT'S JUST BECAUSE I WAS SUPER WORRIED. YOU'RE A BRILLIANT DANCER.

TEN MINUTES LATER...

SUMMER TANBERRY!

GET OUT THERE AND SHOW THEM!

WAS I MISTAKEN FROM THE START? THOSE DANCERS ARE CURVY, THEIR SHOULDERS MUSCLED, LEGS STURDY, THEY'RE NOT WAIFS.

SUMMER, ARE YOU OKAY?

YES...YES, SURE!

THOSE DANCERS AREN'T HUGE OR HIDEOUS. THEY'RE BEAUTIFUL.

HAVE I GOT IT ALL WRONG SOMEHOW?

HELLO, SUMMER! YOUR TURN!

AT THE END OF THE AUDITION...

THANK YOU! I CAN SEE THAT YOU LOVE TO DANCE. SUCH ENERGY, SUCH EMOTION...

WE HAVE JUST THREE SCHOLARSHIPS LEFT TO AWARD. CAN YOU TELL ME WHY YOU DESERVE ONE OF THEM?

I NEED THIS PLACE. IT'S MY DREAM!

LETTERS WILL BE SENT OUT NEXT WEEK...YOU'RE TRULY TALENTED, SUMMER!

I THINK WE CAN SAFELY SAY THAT IT WILL BE GOOD NEWS FOR YOU. YOU'RE A NATURAL.

THANK YOU! THANK YOU! YOU DON'T KNOW WHAT THIS MEANS TO ME!

BACK AT TANGLEWOOD...

WE'RE ALL SO PROUD, SUMMER!

BRAVO!

I'M SURE YOU ROCKED IT!

MISS ELISE ISN'T HERE?

SHE JUST DROPPED ME OFF AND HAD TO GET HOME!

FOR YOU, A CHOCOLATE CAKE EDGED WITH "SUMMER'S DREAM" TRUFFLES!

SUMMER, I'LL CUT YOU THE FIRST SLICE!

MMMMM. THIS IS SO GOOD. HOW COULD SOMETHING THAT TASTES SO GOOD BE SO BAD?

ARE YOU GOING TO LET IT UNRAVEL ALL YOUR HARD WORK? HAVE YOU NO WILLPOWER AT ALL?

IT'S REALLY GOOD... BUT I'M NOT VERY HUNGRY!

YOU'LL MAKE UP FOR IT TONIGHT. WE'VE ORGANIZED A LITTLE BEACH PARTY WITH THE FILM CREW. TOMORROW EVENING, MUM AND PADDY WILL BE HOME. GRANDMA KATE IS LETTING US STAY OUT TILL MIDNIGHT!

TO MY LITTLE SISTER, THE FAMOUS BALLERINA!

HERE, IT'S HARD CIDER. IT'S NOT VERY STRONG!

I CAN'T! I'M THIRTEEN. WHAT ARE YOU PLAYING AT?

I'M TRYING TO LOOSEN YOU UP. IS THAT A CRIME? YOU'RE WOUND SO TIGHT THESE DAYS, YOU'LL SNAP ANY MINUTE!

DANCE ISN'T A PASSION, IT'S YOUR OBSESSION! YOU'RE A MESS AND, TRUST ME, I KNOW WHAT THAT FEELS LIKE. IT TAKES ONE TO KNOW ONE.

LET'S GET ONE THING STRAIGHT. I'M NOT LIKE YOU, NOT ONE LITTLE BIT. I'M NOT A MESS...MY LIFE IS UNDER CONTROL! WHAT'S THE PROBLEM, HONEY, ARE YOU JEALOUS?

ALL RIGHT, COME ON. LET'S DANCE!

WHERE'S COCO?

THINK SHE WENT TO BED. LOOKS LIKE SHE FORGOT HUMBUG!

OKAY, OFF TO THE STABLES, MY PRETTY! COCO MUST HAVE BEEN REALLY SLEEPY. SHE'D NORMALLY NEVER LEAVE YOU.

EEEEEEEEEE!

SHUT UP! YOU'LL WAKE THE WHOLE HOUSE!

YOU SCARED ME HALF TO DEATH!

YOU'RE SMOKING?

SO WHAT? NOT A CRIME IS IT?

OKAY, THEN, I'M GOING BACK TO THE PARTY!

NOW LOOK WHAT YOU'VE DONE. THE FIRST BOY I'VE REALLY LIKED IN AGES!

HE'S NINETEEN. HE'S AN INTERN FOR THE FILM SHOOT. AND IF HE'S SO SPECIAL, HOW COME YOU'VE WRAPPED AROUND JJ ALL EVENING?

YOU'VE BEEN SMOKING! YOU KNOW IT'S REALLY, REALLY BAD FOR YOU!

LISTEN TO YOU! LITTLE MISS PERFECT, LECTURING ME ABOUT THE DANGERS OF SMOKING. WHAT ABOUT THE DANGERS OF ANOREXIA?

44

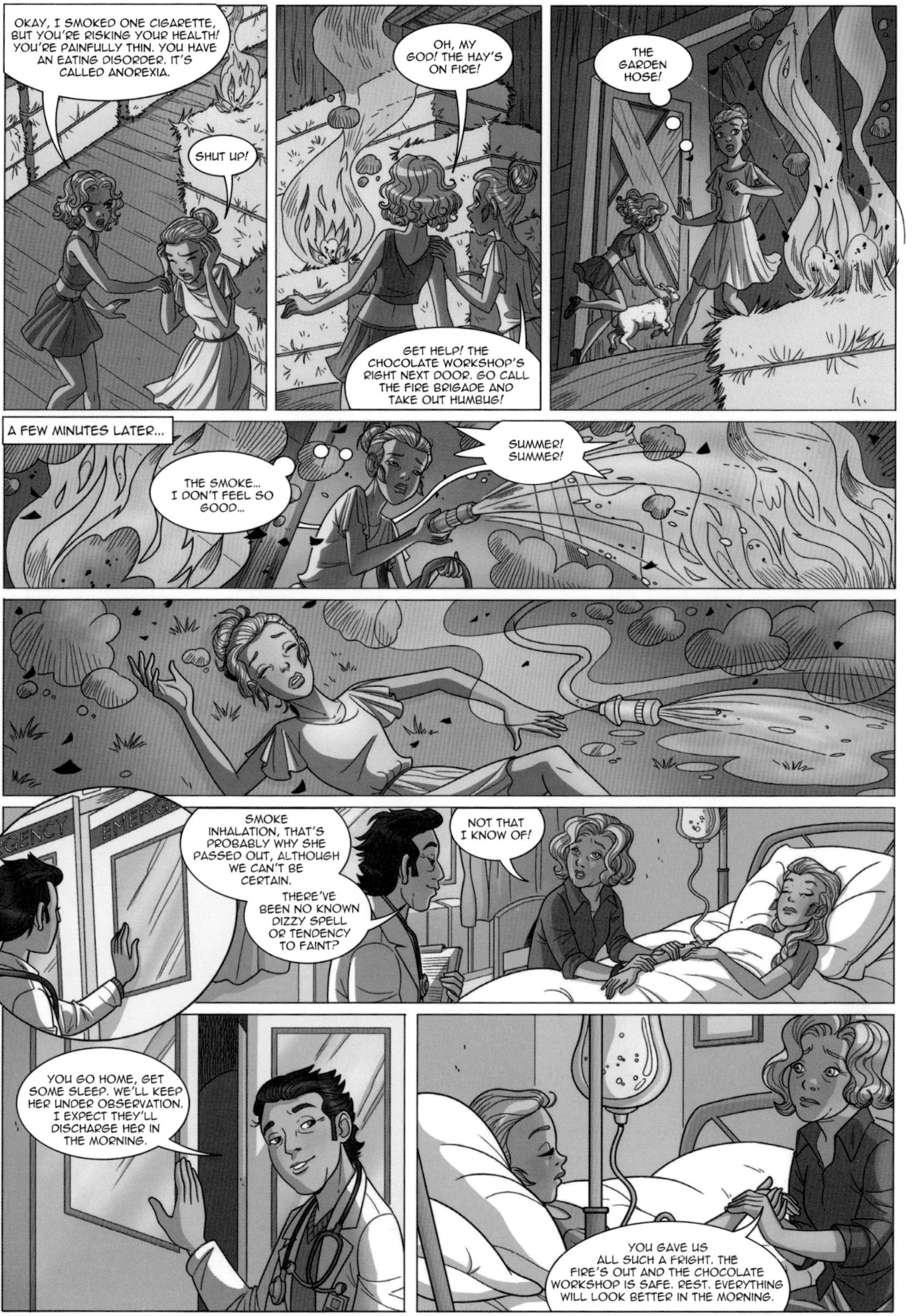
OKAY, I SMOKED ONE CIGARETTE, BUT YOU'RE RISKING YOUR HEALTH! YOU'RE PAINFULLY THIN. YOU HAVE AN EATING DISORDER. IT'S CALLED ANOREXIA.
SHUT UP!
OH, MY GOD! THE HAY'S ON FIRE!
GET HELP! THE CHOCOLATE WORKSHOP'S RIGHT NEXT DOOR. GO CALL THE FIRE BRIGADE AND TAKE OUT HUMBUG!
THE GARDEN HOSE!
A FEW MINUTES LATER...
THE SMOKE... I DON'T FEEL SO GOOD...
SUMMER! SUMMER!
EMERGENCY
SMOKE INHALATION, THAT'S PROBABLY WHY SHE PASSED OUT, ALTHOUGH WE CAN'T BE CERTAIN.
THERE'VE BEEN NO KNOWN DIZZY SPELL OR TENDENCY TO FAINT?
NOT THAT I KNOW OF!
YOU GO HOME, GET SOME SLEEP. WE'LL KEEP HER UNDER OBSERVATION. I EXPECT THEY'LL DISCHARGE HER IN THE MORNING.
YOU GAVE US ALL SUCH A FRIGHT. THE FIRE'S OUT AND THE CHOCOLATE WORKSHOP IS SAFE. REST. EVERYTHING WILL LOOK BETTER IN THE MORNING.

THE NEXT MORNING...

I'M *DR. KHAN*. I SPECIALIZE IN WORKING WITH YOUNG PEOPLE WITH EATING ISSUES. EVERYONE'S QUITE WORRIED ABOUT YOU, YOU KNOW.

YOU DIDN'T FAINT YESTERDAY JUST BECAUSE OF THE SMOKE. YOU'RE WEAK, SUMMER. YOU'RE FEELING WEAK BECAUSE OF YOUR DIET. YOU HAVE ANOREXIA NERVOSA, A VERY SERIOUS PSYCHIATRIC DISORDER. I'M HERE TO HELP YOU...WE'LL SEE EACH OTHER EVERY DAY.

BUT--BUT I WON'T BE ABLE TO GO TO THE BOARDING SCHOOL?

NO! WE HAVE TO TACKLE THIS FIRST... BEATING AN EATING DISORDER TAKES TIME. YOU NEED TO BE PATIENT, DETERMINED. IT'LL BE HARD WORK. BUT IF YOU TRUST ME, I CAN HELP YOU.

I JUST HAD A LONG TALK WITH YOUR PARENTS, WHO JUST GOT BACK FROM THEIR TRIP. I'LL LEAVE YOU WITH THEM!

OH! I FORGOT. YOU HAVE A FRIEND WHO CAME TO SEE YOU, SOMEONE NAMED ALFIE. HE ASKED ME TO GIVE YOU THIS BOUQUET!

I'M SORRY I WASN'T HERE WHEN YOU NEEDED ME. OH, SUMMER, WHAT HAVE YOU DONE TO YOURSELF?

IT'S OKAY, MUM. I'LL GET BETTER!

YOU KNOW HONEY RAN AWAY LAST NIGHT, AFTER ALERTING THE FIRE BRIGADE. THE POLICE FOUND HER AT THE AIRPORT.

SHE TRIED TO BUY A TICKET FOR AUSTRALIA WITH THE EMERGENCY CREDIT CARD TAKEN FROM THE KITCHEN DRAWER.

SHE TOLD US HOW THE BARN CAUGHT FIRE!

SHE MUST BE BLAMING HERSELF!

46

THE NEXT DAY, SUMMER IS OUT OF THE HOSPITAL...

I JUST WANT THINGS TO BE NORMAL. CARRY ON WITH YOUR USUAL THINGS. I'M FINE. I'LL DO EVERYTHING TO GET BETTER, I PROMISE YOU.

I'VE RUINED EVERYTHING AND SABOTAGED MY OWN FUTURE. MUM WILL CALL MISS ELISE AND SYLVIE ROCHELLE.

WE NEED TO TALK.

I'M AN IDIOT. THE WORST BIG SISTER SINCE TIME BEGAN. I'M SO SORRY.

IF I HADN'T DISTURBED YOU, ARGUED WITH YOU, NONE OF THIS WOULD HAVE HAPPENED...

I FAINTED BECAUSE I'D HARDLY EATEN ALL DAY, NOT BECAUSE OF THE SMOKE!

I'VE BEEN WORRIED ABOUT YOU FOR WEEKS. I'M JUST NOT GOOD AT SHOWING IT!

DOCTOR KHAN'S GOING TO HELP ME!

I'VE CROSSED A LINE THIS TIME. SMOKING, STARTING A FIRE, LETTING MY LITTLE SISTER ALMOST BURN TO DEATH...

...I RUN AWAY AND END UP IN A MAJOR POLICE HUNT! I'LL BE GROUNDED UNTIL I'M SIXTY! MY LIFE IS OVER!

NO! WE'LL CHANGE! WE'LL REMOVE THE LABELS PEOPLE HAVE STUCK TO US; YOU THE REBEL, ME LITTLE MISS PERFECT!

WE'RE ON THE RIGHT PATH!

I LOVE YOU, LITTLE SISTER!

ME, TOO!

WE'RE SO DIFFERENT, YET SO ALIKE. I WISH I'D SEEN IT BEFORE.

ALFIE

MEET U ON THE BEACH IN 10 MINUTES, OK?

MUM MENTIONED STUDYING DANCE, TAKING A PERFORMING ARTS COURSE OR TRAINING TO BE A DANCE TEACHER, BUT I CAN'T THINK THAT FAR AHEAD.

YOU CAME!

OF COURSE. YOU ASKED ME TO!

I WON'T BE GOING TO THE ROCHELLE ACADEMY. I NO LONGER EVEN KNOW IF I CARE!

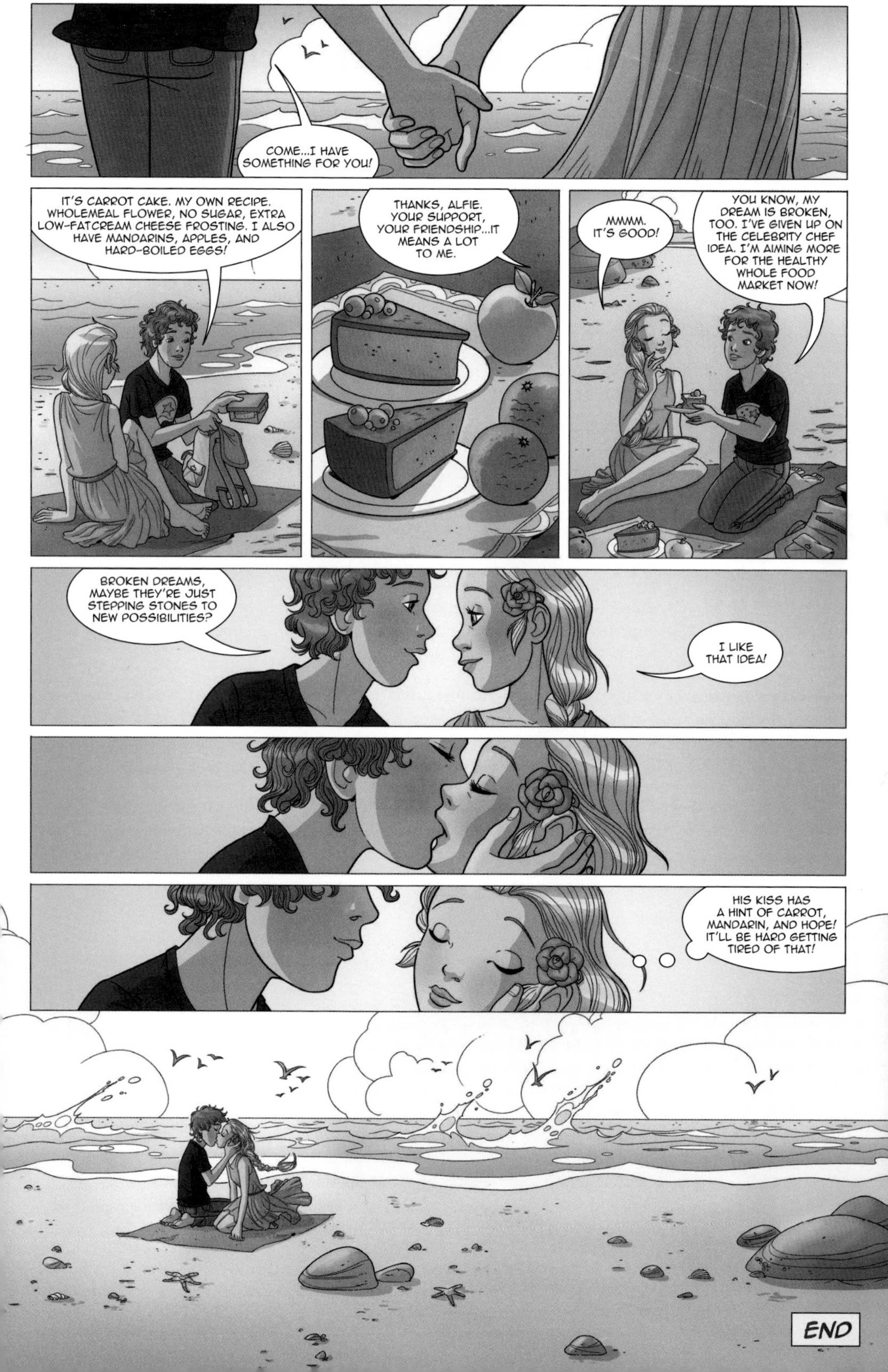
COME...I HAVE SOMETHING FOR YOU!
IT'S CARROT CAKE. MY OWN RECIPE. WHOLEMEAL FLOWER, NO SUGAR, EXTRA LOW-FATCREAM CHEESE FROSTING. I ALSO HAVE MANDARINS, APPLES, AND HARD-BOILED EGGS!
THANKS, ALFIE. YOUR SUPPORT, YOUR FRIENDSHIP...IT MEANS A LOT TO ME.
MMMM. IT'S GOOD!
YOU KNOW, MY DREAM IS BROKEN, TOO. I'VE GIVEN UP ON THE CELEBRITY CHEF IDEA. I'M AIMING MORE FOR THE HEALTHY WHOLE FOOD MARKET NOW!
BROKEN DREAMS, MAYBE THEY'RE JUST STEPPING STONES TO NEW POSSIBILITIES?
I LIKE THAT IDEA!
HIS KISS HAS A HINT OF CARROT, MANDARIN, AND HOPE! IT'LL BE HARD GETTING TIRED OF THAT!
END

About Summer's Problem

In the story you have just read, Summer, a 13-year-old ballet dancer, develops anorexia nervosa. She becomes obsessed about her shape and ballet performance and hears a cruel voice in her head that drives her even harder. She does not eat enough and grows weak, irritable, and tired, and her dancing suffers. She feels alone and unhappy. Summer becomes increasingly sick and ends up in the hospital.

Summer's friends and family express concerns about her, but she ignores them. This is common: many people with eating disorders do not believe they have a problem. This is one reason that when you see a friend who has problems with eating, you should say something. Summer's friend Alfie does the right thing and encourages Summer to talk to an adult. Her sister also tries to confront her about her problem. Only after she passes out and ends up in the hospital does Summer finally get diagnosed with an eating disorder. She sees a doctor and starts to receive treatment.

Eating disorders, including anorexia nervosa, are serious and sometimes deadly medical problems. Dieting is discouraged for young people who are still growing because it can often make a problem worse. Bodies naturally come in all shapes and sizes. If you are concerned about your weight or shape, please talk to your parents or another trusted adult. If you notice a friend showing signs of an eating disorder such as the ones Summer displays—especially refusing to eat—or have other concerns, be like Alfie and try to get your friend to talk to a trusted adult. You cannot cure your friend, but you can help him or her to get professional help.

Also recognize that eating disorders do not just affect teen girls. Eating disorders affect boys as well. In fact, they affect people of all genders, ages, races, ethnicities, body shapes, and weights, sexual orientations, and social classes! And not all people with eating disorders are thin. Eating disorders can occur in people of all shapes and sizes, including people with larger bodies.

What happened to Summer in this story is very frightening. But we can predict that with professional help, hard work, and the love of her family, Summer will make a full recovery. Full recovery from an eating disorder is possible and the chances are increased with early detection and treatment.

— *Lauren Muhlheim,* **PSY.D**

Resources

The National Eating Disorders Association (NEDA) supports individuals and families affected by eating disorders. The association's national toll-free confidential hotline (800-931-2237) is staffed daily by trained volunteers that provide information, support, and referrals to treatment. They also offer 24/7 crisis support via text (send 'NEDA' to 741741), and have many resources on their website for individuals and families.

Proud2Bme.org is an online community created by and for teens and young adults. They cover everything from fashion and beauty to news, culture, and entertainment—all with the goal of promoting positive body image and encouraging healthy attitudes about food and weight.

Sweeties PART TWO "COCO"

THEY SAY THAT FAMILIES ARE LIKE CHOCOLATE -- MOSTLY SWEET, WITH A FEW NUTS. MORE THAN A FEW, IN MY FAMILY'S CASE. MY NAME IS *COCO*. I'M TWELVE AND I'M THE BABY IN A BLENDED FAMILY...

MY FRIENDS THINK MY FAMILY IS COOL, BUT THEY DON'T KNOW THE HALF OF IT. ≑PFF≑ MUM AND PADDY ARE ALWAYS BUSY WITH CHOCOLATE ORDERS...

AS FOR HAVING FOUR SISTERS, WELL, THAT CAN BE SERIOUSLY HARD WORK, ESPECIALLY WHEN YOU'RE THE YOUNGEST.

HONEY LOOKS WELL BEHAVED, BUT SHE'S A REAL TIME BOMB. IT'S LIKE SHE HAS NO LIMITS, NO RULES. SHE'S THE ELDEST, BUT STILL.

SHE RAN AWAY LAST SUMMER. SHE HATES OUR STEPSISTER CHERRY.

NOT TO MENTION SHE'S DATING HONEY'S EX-BOYFRIEND.

51

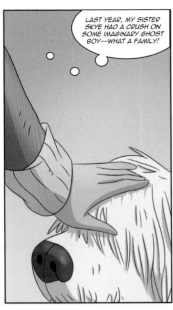

LAST YEAR, MY SISTER SKYE HAD A CRUSH ON SOME IMAGINARY GHOST BOY--WHAT A FAMILY!

AS FOR SUMMER, SKYE'S TWIN, SHE CRACKED UNDER THE PRESSURE OF BECOMING A DANCER. SHE'S ANOREXIC AND STILL STRUGGLING TO BREAK FREE OF IT.

THESE DAYS, SHE'S LIKE A SHADOW GIRL, FRAIL, FRAGILE, LOST. WE HAVE TO PRETEND NOTHING'S WRONG SO WE DON'T PUSH HER TOO HARD.

I KNOW MY SISTERS AREN'T PERFECT, BUT I LOVE THEM.

AND FRED, HUMBUG, I LOVE YOU TWO ALSO. YOU GUYS DON'T CARE WHEN I PLAY THE WRONG NOTES ON MY VIOLIN.

WHEN I GROW UP, I WANT TO WORK WITH ANIMALS. I'LL TRAIN TO BE A VET. I'LL DO VOLUNTEER WORK AND SAVE ENDANGERED SPECIES...

I'M HAVING A CAKE SALE AT SCHOOL ON MONDAY FOR ENDANGERED PANDAS. THAT'S COOL, ISN'T IT?

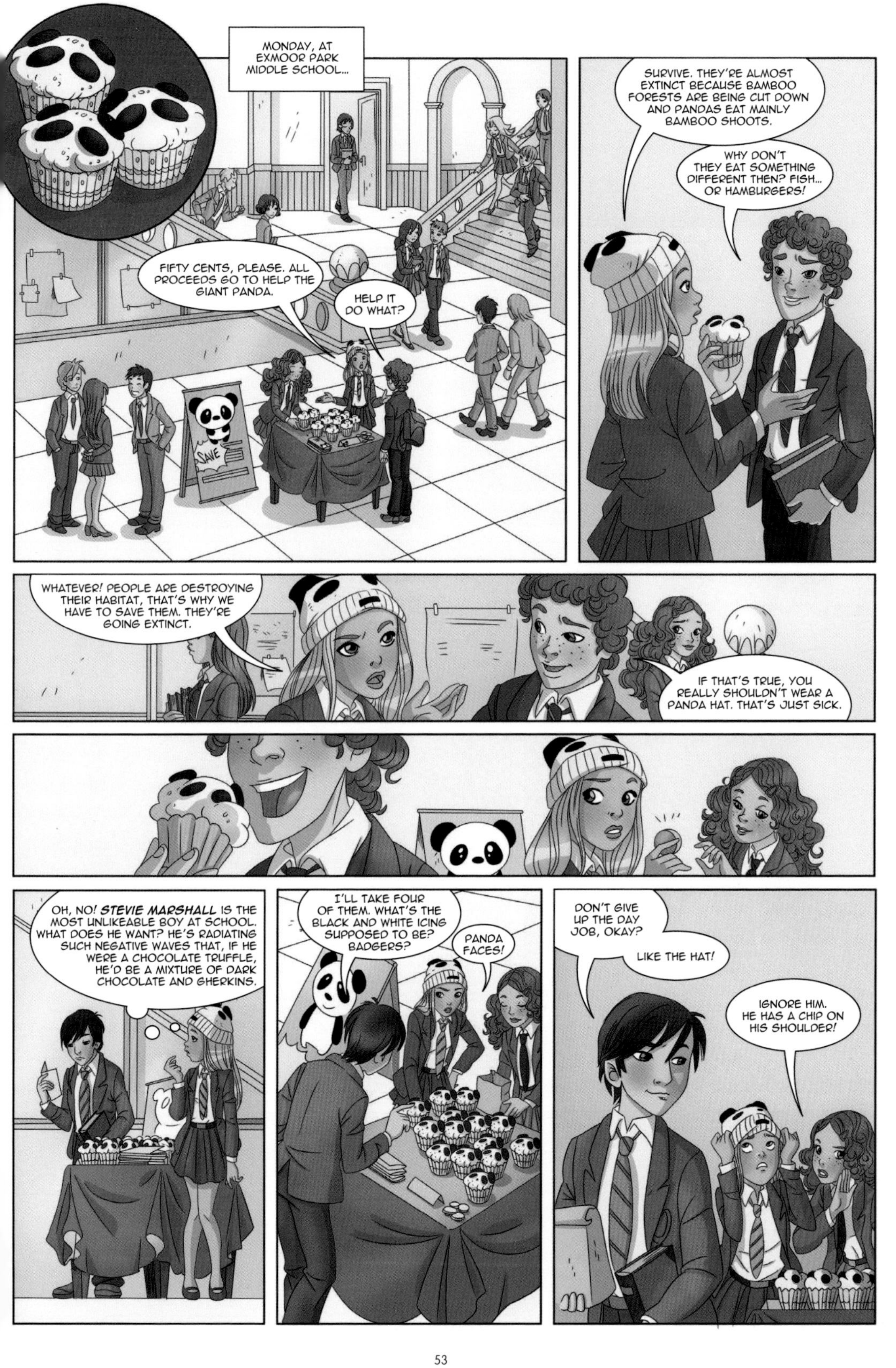

MONDAY, AT EXMOOR PARK MIDDLE SCHOOL...
FIFTY CENTS, PLEASE. ALL PROCEEDS GO TO HELP THE GIANT PANDA.
HELP IT DO WHAT?
SAVE
SURVIVE. THEY'RE ALMOST EXTINCT BECAUSE BAMBOO FORESTS ARE BEING CUT DOWN AND PANDAS EAT MAINLY BAMBOO SHOOTS.
WHY DON'T THEY EAT SOMETHING DIFFERENT THEN? FISH... OR HAMBURGERS!
WHATEVER! PEOPLE ARE DESTROYING THEIR HABITAT, THAT'S WHY WE HAVE TO SAVE THEM. THEY'RE GOING EXTINCT.
IF THAT'S TRUE, YOU REALLY SHOULDN'T WEAR A PANDA HAT. THAT'S JUST SICK.
OH, NO! ***STEVIE MARSHALL*** IS THE MOST UNLIKEABLE BOY AT SCHOOL. WHAT DOES HE WANT? HE'S RADIATING SUCH NEGATIVE WAVES THAT, IF HE WERE A CHOCOLATE TRUFFLE, HE'D BE A MIXTURE OF DARK CHOCOLATE AND GHERKINS.
I'LL TAKE FOUR OF THEM. WHAT'S THE BLACK AND WHITE ICING SUPPOSED TO BE? BADGERS?
PANDA FACES!
DON'T GIVE UP THE DAY JOB, OKAY?
LIKE THE HAT!
IGNORE HIM. HE HAS A CHIP ON HIS SHOULDER!

AFTER SCHOOL...

THAT'S COOL. WE MADE A LITTLE MONEY EARLIER. THAT'LL PLANT A LOT OF BAMBOO.

I CAN'T FIND MY PANDA HAT!

I MUST'VE LEFT IT IN CLASS. DON'T WAIT FOR ME, *SARAH*. I'LL SEE YOU TOMORROW.

OKAY!

WHO WOULD DO SUCH A THING?

I'M SURE IT WAS STEVIE MARSHALL. HE MADE A COMMENT ABOUT MY HAT EARLIER.

STEVIE'S THE ONE WHO'LL BE AN ENDANGERED SPECIES IF I SEE HIM!

54

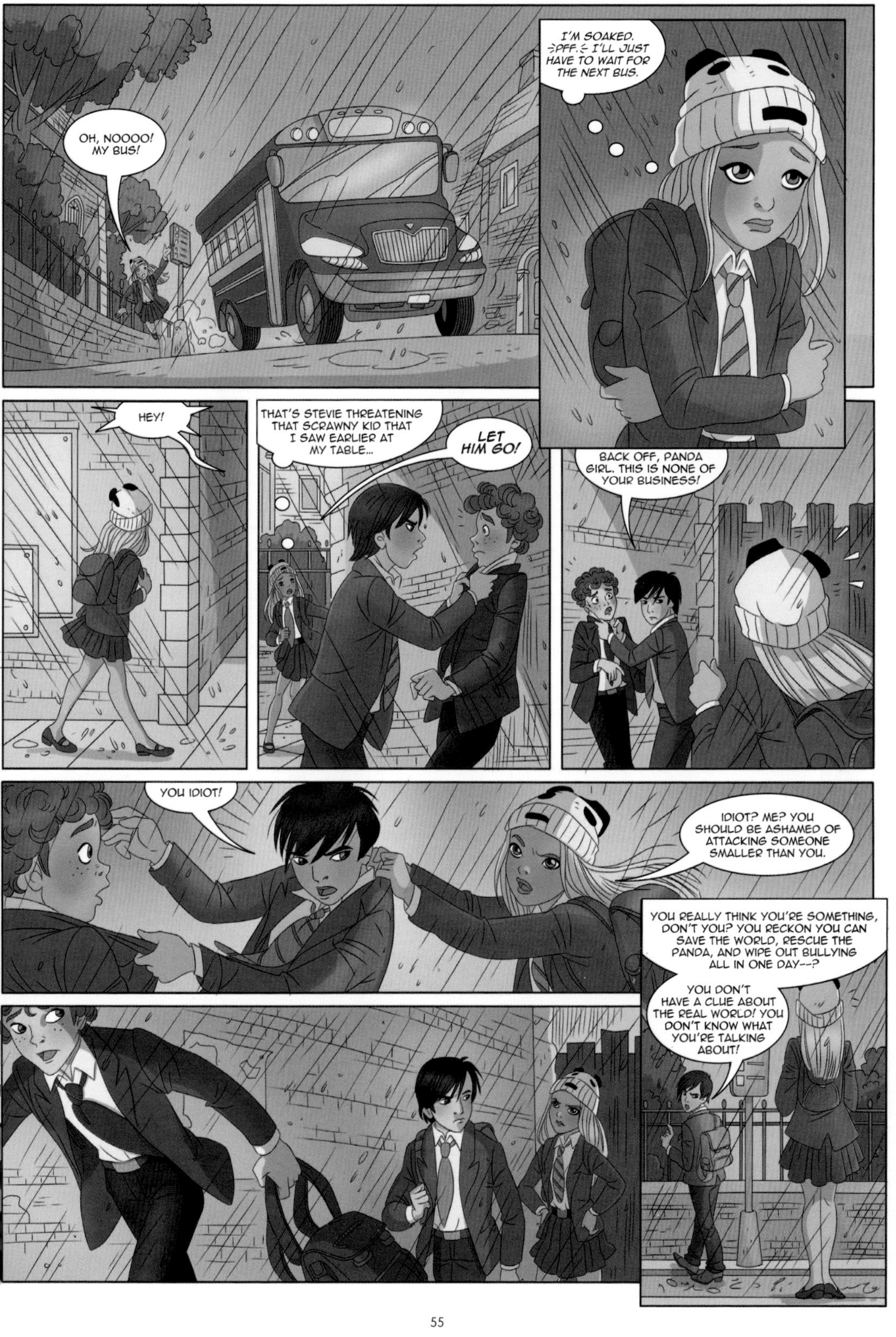

OH, NOOOO! MY BUS!
I'M SOAKED. ≈PFF.≈ I'LL JUST HAVE TO WAIT FOR THE NEXT BUS.
HEY!
THAT'S STEVIE THREATENING THAT SCRAWNY KID THAT I SAW EARLIER AT MY TABLE...
LET HIM GO!
BACK OFF, PANDA GIRL. THIS IS NONE OF YOUR BUSINESS!
YOU IDIOT!
IDIOT? ME? YOU SHOULD BE ASHAMED OF ATTACKING SOMEONE SMALLER THAN YOU.
YOU REALLY THINK YOU'RE SOMETHING, DON'T YOU? YOU RECKON YOU CAN SAVE THE WORLD, RESCUE THE PANDA, AND WIPE OUT BULLYING ALL IN ONE DAY--?
YOU DON'T HAVE A CLUE ABOUT THE REAL WORLD! YOU DON'T KNOW WHAT YOU'RE TALKING ABOUT!

THE FOLLOWING FRIDAY...

ARE YOU OKAY? HE HASN'T BOTHERED YOU AGAIN, HAS HE?

ER... NO. AND YES, THANKS, I'M FINE. NO WORRIES.

YOU MUSTN'T LET YOURSELF BE MISTREATED. YOU SHOULD TELL THE GUIDANCE COUNSELOR. IF YOU DON'T, STEVIE MIGHT DO IT AGAIN.

IT'S OKAY, I'VE SORTED IT OUT NOW. AND--LOOK-- I'M SORRY ABOUT THE HAT!

THAT WAS THE KID STEVIE MARSHALL HAD A HOLD OF THE OTHER DAY?

WHAT DID HE MEAN ABOUT MY HAT?

HE DOESN'T LOOK LIKE A VICTIM. MORE OF A TROUBLEMAKER. MAYBE HE'S THE ONE WHO HOISTED YOUR HAT UP THE FLAGPOLE!

NO, THAT HAD TO BE STEVIE. HE MADE FUN OF ME, THAT'S FOR SURE.

I'M OUT OF SORTS ALL DAY AFTER THAT. LUCKILY, I HAVE A RIDING LESSON AFTER SCHOOL. I'VE BEEN LEARNING TO RIDE SINCE CHRISTMAS AND I LOVE IT! MOST OF ALL, THOUGH, I LOVE A PONY CALLED *CARAMEL*. SHE'S A PUREBRED EXMOOR, TWELVE HANDS HIGH. SHE LOOKS TIMELESS, NOBLE, AND MAGICAL. SHE'S THE PONY OF MY DREAMS.

I KNOW YOU WANT TO RIDE HER, COCO, BUT YOU KNOW SHE'S HARD TO CONTROL. SHE'S JUMPY AND UNPREDICTABLE.

YES, I KNOW YOU HAVE TO BE EXPERIENCED TO RIDE HER, BUT-- PLEASE!

SHE LIKES YOU, THAT'S OBVIOUS. AND THAT'S NOT THE CASE WITH EVERYONE. BUT NO WAY!

ALL RIGHT, COME AND WORK IN THE PADDOCK. I'LL GET *BAILEY*, THE GENTLEST OF THE PONIES, READY FOR YOU.

WHAT ARE *YOU* DOING HERE?

I'M HERE FOR MY RIDING LESSON. WHAT ARE YOU DOING HERE?

I WORK HERE, THREE FORTY-FIVE TILL SIX, TUESDAYS AND FRIDAYS. IT'S MY FIRST DAY.

IF I'D KNOWN THEY GAVE LESSONS TO FRUITCAKES LIKE YOU, I MIGHT'VE HAD SECOND THOUGHTS.

FRUITCAKE TO YOU, TOO!

AS COMEBACKS GO, THAT WASN'T THE BEST. I'M SO LAME!

I DO NOT LIKE THAT BOY.

ARE YOU COMING, COCO? THE OTHER STUDENTS ARE HERE. WE'RE WAITING ON YOU!

I REALLY CAN'T RIDE CARAMEL? I'VE MADE A LOT OF PROGRESS!

NO. *JEAN* AND *ROY** AREN'T HERE TODAY AND THAT PONY CAN BE UNPREDICTABLE.

JEAN PROMISED ME THAT I COULD RIDE HER, *KELLY*. PLEASE LET ME TRY. WE'LL STAY IN THE PADDOCK!

* JEAN AND ROY ARE THE DIRECTORS OF THE RIDING SCHOOL.

PLEASE!

WHAT IF IT GOES BAD?

IT WON'T!

WELL, OKAY! STEVIE, CAN YOU GET CARAMEL SADDLED UP, PLEASE? FOR COCO HERE.

I THOUGHT YOU SAID ONLY EXPERIENCED RIDERS COULD TAKE CARAMEL?

I'M AN EXPERIENCED RIDER, YOU KNOW.

FIFTEEN MINUTES LATER...

OKAY. RISING TROT.

I KNOW CARAMEL AND I WILL GET ALONG WONDERFULLY.

THAT'S GOOD... GALLOP NOW!

HEY!

HOW COULD YOU DO THIS TO ME? I THOUGHT WE HAD AN UNDERSTANDING.

COCO, ARE YOU ALL RIGHT?

OUCH... YES, YES... OUCH!

I'M EMBARRASSED. THIS IS THE MOST HUMILIATING MOMENT OF MY LIFE.

YOU'RE LIMPING? WHAT HAPPENED TO YOU?

I HAD AN ARGUMENT WITH MY FAVORITE PONY. SHE GOT TIRED OF BEHAVING BEAUTIFULLY AND DECIDED TO THROW ME OFF.

SERIOUSLY? WHAT KIND OF PSYCHO HORSES DO THEY HAVE AT THAT PLACE?

IT'S SUPPOSED TO BE A RIDING SCHOOL NOT A RODEO.

DON'T. IT'S TAKEN ME THE WHOLE DRIVE HOME TO CONVINCE MUM NOT TO LODGE A COMPLAINT.

I DON'T WANT TO COMPLAIN. I JUST WANTED TO SAY THAT PONY REALLY SHOULDN'T BE PART OF A RIDING SCHOOL. SHE'S TOO WILD!

MUM, I TOLD YOU IT WAS ALL MY OWN FAULT.

IS THERE A PROBLEM?

YES!

I DIDN'T HAVE PERMISSION TO RIDE CARAMEL, BUT SHE'S MY FAVORITE PONY. AND JEAN AND ROY WEREN'T THERE. I BEGGED KELLY TO LET ME RIDE HER.

IN SHORT, YOU LIED.

GOOD THING YOU HAD YOUR HELMET ON, BABY SISTER. YOU MIGHT HAVE DONE SOME REAL DAMAGE.

I JUST HAVE SOME SCRAPES AND A BRUISE.

YOU'RE THE BABY OF THE FAMILY TO US. WE WORRY ABOUT YOU.

WELL, DON'T. I'M NOT A BABY ANYMORE. YOU AND SKYE ARE ONLY SEVENTEEN MONTHS OLDER THAN I AM.

OKAY, COCO, GO TAKE A SHOWER WHILE I TAKE A CUP OF TEA TO PADDY IN THE WORKSHOP.

IT'S NOT YOU I'M WORRYING ABOUT REALLY, COCO, IT'S HONEY. I THOUGHT SHE'D SETTLED DOWN AFTER RUNNING AWAY LAST SUMMER...

MY ART TEACHER ASKED ME TODAY WHEN HONEY WOULD BE BACK TO SCHOOL--

WHAT? HONEY IS SKIPPING SCHOOL?

THEY ALL THINK SHE'S ILL.

SHE TAKES THE SCHOOL BUS WITH US EVERY DAY--

OKAY. SHE MAY BE ON THE BUS, BUT SHE OBVIOUSLY ISN'T MAKING IT PAST THE GATES, AND AFTERWARDS SHE MUST GO INTO TOWN.

WAIT TILL MUM FINDS OUT... SHE'LL GO NUTS!

SHE WILL!

REPORT CARDS ARE OUT NEXT WEDNESDAY. MUM WILL FIND OUT THEN. SO WE WON'T SAY ANYTHING.

ON WEDNESDAY, MY CHIN IS ALMOST HEALED AND THE BRUISES ON MY LEGS HAVE FADED TO RAINBOW SHADES OF BLUE, PURPLE, AND GREENISH-YELLOW. THEY LOOK ESPECIALLY ATTRACTIVE WITH MY GYM SHORTS, AND I HAVE TO RECOUNT THE STORY OF HOW THE UNPREDICTABLE, HALF-WILD PONY GOT STARTLED AND THREW ME OFF...

YOU HAVE TO GET USED TO THESE THINGS WHEN YOU MOVE ON TO RIDING MORE CHALLENGING HORSES, BUT THEY'RE THE MOST REWARDING ONES, OF COURSE.

PLEASED WITH YOURSELF?

PLEASED ABOUT WHAT?

YOU DON'T EVEN KNOW? YOU DON'T EVEN CARE?

WHAT A LOSER. HOW COME HE ALWAYS MANAGES TO MAKE ME FEEL LIKE I'M THE ONE WHO'S DONE SOMETHING WRONG?

A LITTLE QUIET, PLEASE! TAKE OUT YOUR NOTEBOOKS.

YOU'RE PROBABLY THE MOST SPOILED, SELFISH GIRL I'VE EVER MET. YOU LIED ABOUT BEING ALLOWED TO RIDE CARAMEL, DIDN'T YOU?

NO, I--

BECAUSE OF YOU, KELLY GOT IN TROUBLE, AND JEAN AND ROY ARE SELLING CARAMEL. IT'S ALL YOUR FAULT.

WHAT?!

QUIET, I SAID!

NO, THIS CAN'T BE POSSIBLE-- CARAMEL--

LATER, AFTER SCHOOL...

YOU ARE THE DANCING QUEEN...YOUNG AND SWEET...

SO, THIS IS WHAT YOU GET UP TO WHEN WE'RE AT SCHOOL?

OH, COCO, LOVE, WE'RE CELEBRATING!

YOUR THREE-MONTH ANNIVERSARY? A LOTTERY WIN?

ALMOST...

WE'VE JUST LANDED A MAJOR ORDER FROM THE MILLER-BROWN CHAIN OF DEPARTMENT STORES!

THEY'VE OFFERED US THE CHANCE TO SUPPLY FIFTY OF THEIR TOP STORES! EVERYONE WILL BE SNAPPING UP OUR TRUFFLES!

WOW!

ALL THE CHOCOLATES PADDY INVENTED FOR YOU WILL BE THERE: CHERRY CRUSH, MARSHMALLOW SKYE, SUMMER'S DREAM, COCO CARAMEL, AND SWEET HONEY.

ARE WE GOING TO BE RICH? ENOUGH TO BUY A PONY, SAY?

A PONY?

MUM, THE STABLES ARE SELLING CARAMEL! IT'S ALL MY FAULT, AND I THOUGHT IF WE COULD JUST BUY HER--

RICH? I WOULDN'T GO THAT FAR. WE SHOULD BE ABLE TO PAY OFF OUR BUSINESS LOANS, AT ANY RATE.

MUM... PLEASE...TO SAVE CARAMEL.

WE'LL TALK ABOUT IT LATER. DON'T GET YOUR HOPES UP.

YOU ARE THE DANCING QUEEN...YOUNG AND SWEET...

WHAT'S THE PARTY?

BETTER GET IT OVER WITH, I KNOW IT WON'T BE GOOD, BUT I HAVE BEEN TRYING A LOT HARDER, SO--

MUM AND PADDY LAUNCH INTO THE STORY OF THE BIG ORDER AGAIN, BEFORE OPENING THE REPORT CARDS IN THE BIG BROWN ENVELOPES. HONEY WAITS AS LONG AS SHE CAN BEAR, THEN FLINGS HERS DOWN, AS IF THROWING DOWN A CHALLENGE...

SHE'S GOING TO GET AN EARFUL, SEEING AS HOW SHE'S SKIPPING SCHOOL. SHE DOESN'T LOOK TOO FREAKED OUT?

HONEY, THIS IS THE BEST REPORT CARD YOU'VE EVER BROUGHT HOME. WELL DONE! I'M SO PROUD OF YOU, SWEETIE!

?

MUCH IMPROVED ATTITUDE, WORKING HARD TO MAKE UP FOR LOST TIME--NO ABSENCES FROM CLASS.

MAYBE THE ART TEACHER HAD HONEY MIXED UP WITH SOMEONE ELSE?

OUR TURN!

THERE'S SOMETHING STRANGE GOING ON, ISN'T THERE?

THE NEXT DAY, AT THE RIDING SCHOOL...

MUM, WILL YOU ASK JEAN AND ROY ABOUT CARAMEL. IT WOULD BE SO AWESOME IF YOU BOUGHT HER!

COCO, I'VE ALREADY TOLD YOU THAT'S NOT A DECISION YOU MAKE OVERNIGHT. WE HAVE TO THINK.

WHO IS THAT MAN? THE VETERINARIAN?

HELLO, KELLY!

HAVE YOU SEEN STEVIE? I'VE BEEN LOOKING EVERYWHERE FOR HIM.

JEAN AND ROY WANTED STEVIE TO BRING CARAMEL DOWN TO THE PADDOCK, BUT I EXPECT THEY'LL MANAGE THEMSELVES.

I CAN TAKE CARAMEL DOWN TO THE PADDOCK, IF YOU LIKE. I COULD FILL IN FOR STEVIE.

NOT A CHANCE! YOU'RE NOT ALLOWED ANYWHERE NEAR CARAMEL. YOU WEREN'T TRUTHFUL WITH ME LAST WEEK, WERE YOU?

COME ON. LET'S TAKE A WALK INTO THE WOODS.

FIFTEEN MINUTES LATER...

I'M SORRY. I REALLY DIDN'T MEAN TO GET YOU INTO TROUBLE...I WAS TRYING TO SHOW THAT MY FAVORITE PONY WAS GOOD AND STEADY WHEN I RODE HER THE OTHER DAY.

THINGS DIDN'T QUITE WORK OUT THEN, DID THEY? THAT MAN WHO'S THERE WITH HIS VAN, *MR. SEDDON*, IS GOING TO BUY HER. HE'S RICH... HE HAS A BIG HOUSE WITH PADDOCKS AND STABLES.

DON'T WORRY, SHE'LL HAVE A GOOD LIFE.

CARAMEL HAS BEEN SOLD...OH, NOOOOO!

I DIDN'T EVEN GET TO TELL HER GOODBYE.

64

WELL DONE! THANKS TO YOU, CARAMEL BELONGS TO THAT THUG SEDDON NOW.

KELLY SAYS HE'S RICH AND KNOWS LOADS ABOUT HORSES. CARAMEL WILL HAVE A GOOD LIFE WITH HIM.

SHE OBVIOUSLY DOESN'T KNOW HIM!

WHAT DO YOU MEAN, HE'S A THUG?

I JUST KNOW, ALL RIGHT?

YOU DON'T LIKE BULLIES, DO YOU?

OBVIOUSLY. NOBODY LIKES THEM!

WELL, A BULLY IS EXACTLY WHAT SEDDON IS. WITH ANIMALS, WITH PEOPLE, WITH EVERYONE.

NOW, LEAVE ME ALONE.

LATER, AT TANGLEWOOD...

MAYBE YOU COULD CALL JEAN AND ROY, EXPLAIN THAT WE'RE STILL INTERESTED IN CARAMEL?

COCO, LOVE, EVERYTHING WILL BE FINE FOR HER. I'D LOVE FOR YOU TO HAVE A PONY ONE DAY, BUT NOT THAT ONE.

SATURDAY, IN THE EARLY AFTERNOON...

I HAVE TO FIND OUT HOW MY PONY'S DOING AT MR. SEDDON'S.

DON'T SCREW UP MY COMPUTER, OKAY?

YEAH...HEY! YOU COULD KNOCK BEFORE YOU COME IN.

SEDDON... THERE HE IS! THERE'S ONLY ONE ENTRY: J. SEDDON AT BLUE DOWNS HOUSE, HARTSHILL.

THAT'S ABOUT FIVE OR SIX MILES FROM HERE. I HAVE TO GO THERE!

FIVE MINUTES LATER...

I MIGHT CYCLE UP TO TOWN TO SEE SARAH. I WON'T BE LATE.

OKAY, BE CAREFUL!

THERE IT IS!

MY PONY!

NO, NOT THE CROP! YOU'LL HURT HER.

OH, NO-- WHAT A BRUTE!

PLEASE! LEAVE HER ALONE!

SHE HAS TO LEARN. SHE NEEDS DISCIPLINE!

YOU'RE HURTING HER! SHE'S SCARED!

THIS IS HOW IT WORKS, *JASMINE*. ANIMALS NEED TO KNOW WHO IS MASTER.

YOU WANTED A PONY. SO LET ME SEE TO IT.

HAVE TO HIDE, OR I'LL BE SPOTTED. I CAN'T DO ANYTHING. THAT MAN MAKES ME WANT TO VOMIT.

CARAMEL IS SUFFERING. ⇥SNFF!⇤

 CARAMEL'S NEW LIFE ISN'T AT ALL WHAT I'D PICTURED--

 STOP CRYING!

SHOULD I CALL THE SPCA*?

 I CAN'T RISK LEAVING CARAMEL HERE. I HAVE TO GET HER OUT, BUT HOW?

 I'LL CALL CHERRY. SHE'S THE ONLY ONE WHO TAKES ME SERIOUSLY IN THIS FAMILY.

COCO

6:30

 COCO? WHAT'S GOING ON?

 I NEED YOU TO COVER FOR ME. IT'S REALLY IMPORTANT. LIFE AND DEATH. I NEED YOU TO TELL MUM AND PADDY I'M STAYING OVER WITH SARAH.

 YOU'RE NOT WITH HER, IF I UNDERSTOOD CORRECTLY. WHERE WILL YOU SLEEP?

I'LL BE COMING HOME, BUT IT'LL BE VERY LATE, AND I DON'T WANT MUM TO WORRY. I'LL SLEEP IN THE CARAVAN. I'LL EXPLAIN EVERYTHING LATER.

*SOCIETY FOR THE PREVENTION OF CRUELTY TO ANIMALS.

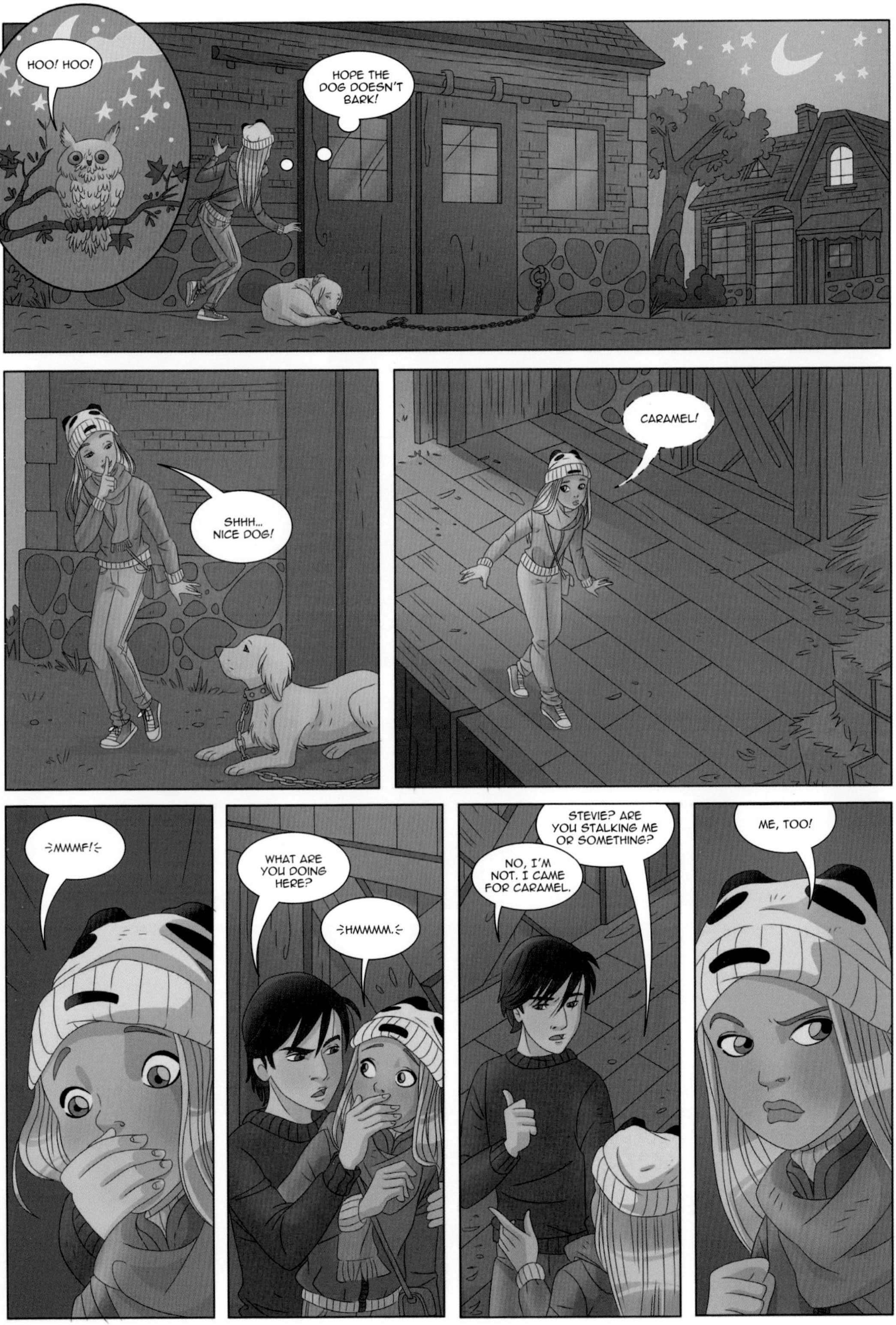
HOO! HOO!
HOPE THE DOG DOESN'T BARK!
SHHH... NICE DOG!
CARAMEL!
≑MMMF!≑
WHAT ARE YOU DOING HERE?
≑HMMMM.≑
STEVIE? ARE YOU STALKING ME OR SOMETHING?
NO, I'M NOT. I CAME FOR CARAMEL.
ME, TOO!

YOU WERE RIGHT ABOUT SEDDON. I WATCHED HIM EARLIER, RUNNING CARAMEL IN THE PADDOCK. HE'S HORRIBLE! DO YOU THINK WE SHOULD CALL THE SPCA?

NO! YOU HAVE NO IDEA HOW POWERFUL HE IS. HE OWNS LOTS OF LAND AROUND HERE, KNOWS ALL THE RIGHT PEOPLE. THERE'S NOT MUCH WE CAN DO.

YES! WE'LL RESCUE HER. STEAL HER. TAKE HER FAR AWAY. WILL YOU HELP ME?

STEAL HER? ARE YOU SERIOUS?

WE CAN'T LEAVE HER HERE.

WHY NOT? SEDDON LIED TO GET HER. JEAN AND ROY WOULD NEVER HAVE LET HER GO IF THEY'D KNOWN WHAT A CREEP HE IS.

WE HAVE TO SAVE THIS OTHER HORSE, TOO. SHE'S IN FOAL.*

SEDDON BOUGHT HER CHEAP AND HE'S TOTALLY NEGLECTED HER.

HOO! HOO!

WHERE ARE WE GOING?

YOU'LL SEE!

THEY SHOULD BE OKAY HERE. IT'S AN OLD, ABANDONED HOUSE.

THERE'S NO PROPER ROAD TO IT...

NOBODY WOULD THINK OF LOOKING THERE.

*PREGNANT.

I WAKE UP LATE, SHIVERING UNDER THE QUILT IN THE CARAVAN. FRED THE DOG SLEPT BESIDE ME. THE DOOR OPENS, AND CHERRY COMES IN WITH FRENCH TOAST AND HOT CHOCOLATE...

ROOM SERVICE!

OH! THANKS, CHERRY!

YOU'RE OFFICIALLY THE BEST STEPSISTER I'VE EVER HAD.

I'M THE ONLY STEPSISTER YOU'VE EVER HAD. I WAS WORRIED SICK! TELL ME WHAT YOU WERE DOING, COCO, PLEASE?

PROMISE YOU WON'T SAY ANYTHING TO ANYONE?

I GUESS, BUT IT'S NOTHING AWFUL, IS IT? NOTHING ILLEGAL?

OKAY, I'LL START FROM THE BEGINNING. CARAMEL...SEDDON...

AFTER TELLING HER THE WHOLE STORY...

BUT SEDDON WILL REPORT THE THEFT TO THE POLICE. AND WHO'S THIS STEVIE YOU'RE TALKING ABOUT? YOUR BOYFRIEND?

NO WAY! HE'S THE MOST ARROGANT BOY THAT I KNOW. HE CAME TO THE SCHOOL LAST SPRING. BEFORE THAT HE LIVED IN NORTHERN ENGLAND. HE'S NOT VERY TALKATIVE...BUT HE LOVES ANIMALS LIKE I DO.

YOU'VE RESCUED THE PONIES, AND THAT'S GREAT, BUT I THINK YOU SHOULD TELL THE AUTHORITIES NOW. YOU SHOULDN'T GET IN TOO DEEP!

I'M ALREADY IN TOO DEEP, AND THERE'S NO TURNING BACK.

71

HMM. THE LITTLE GIRL AT SEDDON'S WAS CALLED JASMINE, TOO.

JASMINE COTTAGE

DANGER. UNSAFE BUILDING

LYING LIKE THIS, IT'S LIKE I'M TURNING INTO A MINI-VERSION OF HONEY. I SAID I WAS GOING TO SEE MY FRIENDS. IT'S A GOOD THING MUM AND PADDY ARE OVERWHELMED WITH WORK IN THE SHOP WITH THEIR BIG ORDER. THAT'LL GIVE ME TIME.

I BROUGHT YOU SOME TREATS. CARROTS, AND APPLE SLICES.

HI.

OH! I DIDN'T SEE YOU.

IS IT REALLY SAFE TO LEAVE THE PONIES HERE?

I THINK SO. I'VE BEEN UP HERE TONS OF TIMES OVER THE SUMMER AND NEVER SEEN ANOTHER SOUL.

WE'LL HAVE TO GET ORGANIZED TO FEED THEM. WE'LL COME AFTER SCHOOL. I'LL COME UP ON TUESDAYS AND FRIDAYS, AFTER WORK AT THE RIDING SCHOOL. BUT ON SATURDAYS, I CAN'T. I HAVE TO TAKE MY LITTLE SISTER TO DANCE CLASS.

I DIDN'T KNOW YOU HAD A LITTLE SISTER.

YES, SHE'S EIGHT. UH--I MEANT TO TELL YOU. THE OTHER DAY IN THE ALLEY WITH *DARREN*. I WAS GIVING HIM A LESSON FOR BULLYING OTHERS. HE'S THE ONE WHO HOISTED YOUR PANDA HAT UP THE SCHOOL FLAGPOLE.

OH! I'M SORRY! I GOT IT ALL WRONG.

ON MONDAY AT LUNCHTIME, I CALL AN EMERGENCY MEETING OF THE SAVE THE ANIMALS CLUB. I DRAG SARAH, *AMY*, AND *JADE* DOWN TO THE EDGE OF THE PLAYING FIELDS AND INTO THE WOODS THAT SKIRT THE SCHOOL GROUNDS.

IF YOU'VE BROUGHT US OUT HERE TO START TELLING US ABOUT THE SOUTH AMERICAN GREAT CRESTED NEWT OR THE SIBERIAN MONGOOSE, I WON'T BE HAPPY!

WE COULD'VE STAYED IN THE STUDY HALL.

YEAH. JADE'S RIGHT. IT'S FREEZING.

I'M NOT ACTUALLY SURE THERE ARE GREAT CRESTED NEWTS IN SOUTH AMERICA, BUT ANYWAY, IT'S NOTHING LIKE THAT. I HAVE BIG NEWS!

I HAPPEN TO KNOW THAT LOCAL ANIMAL RIGHTS ACTIVISTS RESCUED TWO MISTREATED PONIES FROM THE PROPERTY OF A CERTAIN MR. SEDDON.

WOW!

MIGHT THESE LOCAL ACTIVISTS ACTUALLY BE YOU, COCO?

WELL... SORT OF!

NO WAY! YOU RESCUED TWO PONIES?

I HAD TO. THEY WERE BEING MISTREATED... ANYONE WOULD HAVE DONE THE SAME.

THIS HAS TO STAY SECRET. I CAN TRUST YOU, RIGHT?

OF COURSE, WE WON'T BREATHE A WORD!

OH! ALL RIGHT, I WON'T TELL THEM STEVIE WAS WITH ME.

WOW, COCO, I JUST CAN'T BELIEVE YOU DID THAT, ALL BY YOURSELF!

HELLO, STEVIE!

HI!

HE SPOKE TO YOU! STEVIE MARSHALL SPOKE TO YOU...WOW!

AND YOU SPOKE TO HIM. WHAT'S GOING ON? I THOUGHT YOU COULDN'T STAND HIM!

I'VE DECIDED NOT TO LET HIM GET TO ME...

...THE MORE HE SCOWLS, THE NICER I'LL BE WITH HIM!

YOU'RE RIGHT. THAT'S A GOOD STRATEGY.

HE'S NOT BAD. DARK AND BROODING. SORT OF WILD!

THE HERO IN THE BOOK I'M READING IS EXACTLY THE SAME. MOODY AND MYSTERIOUS, BUT WITH HIDDEN DEPTHS. MAYBE STEVIE WILL ASK YOU OUT.

YOU LIKE HIM, I CAN TELL.

OF COURSE NOT! REALLY, HE'S NOT INTERESTED...AND NEITHER AM I.

INSTANTLY, THE PONY RESCUE IS OLD NEWS, REPLACED BY A FRENZIED FASCINATION FOR WHETHER I'M CRUSHING ON STEVIE. WHY'S EVERYONE OBSESSED WITH BOYS ALL OF A SUDDEN? IT'S LIKE THE MINUTE WE TURNED TWELVE, THAT'S ALL ANYONE CAN THINK ABOUT.

THEY DON'T SUSPECT FOR A SINGLE SECOND THAT I'M SPENDING MOST OF MY AFTERNOONS AT THE OLD COTTAGE WITH HIM...

I SEE HIM GETTING OUT OF A VERY POSH FOUR-WHEEL DRIVE SOME MORNINGS, SO HE CAN'T EXACTLY BE POOR!

HMMMMM, WHAT A MYSTERIOUS BOY, THAT STEVIE.

OKAY, LET'S HURRY, WE'RE GOING TO BE LATE!

LATER THAT AFTERNOON...

I HEAR SEDDON'S BEEN TO THE POLICE. THEY'RE MAKING INQUIRIES, PLANNING A SEARCH.

OH, NO! THEY MUSTN'T FIND THE PONIES.

JASMIN COTTA

IT'S NOT LIKELY. THE COTTAGE IS VERY ISOLATED, BUT I'M WORRIED ABOUT THE MARE THAT'S GOING TO FOAL.

DON'T WORRY ABOUT THAT. I'M GOING TO BE A VET, REMEMBER? DELIVERING A FOAL WOULD BE NO PROBLEM AT ALL.

LET'S JUST HOPE SHE DOESN'T FOAL TOO SOON. SHE'S WEAK AND, IF WE CALL A VET, HE'LL TURN US OVER TO SEDDON.

DON'T BE SO PESSIMISTIC!

WAKE UP, WILL YOU? AND OPEN YOUR EYES! NOT EVERYTHING IN LIFE HAS A HAPPY ENDING. NOT EVERYTHING THAT'S BROKEN CAN BE FIXED.

WHAT IF WE'VE MADE EVERYTHING WORSE FOR CARAMEL AND THE MARE? HAVE YOU THOUGHT OF THAT?

TWO DAYS LATER...

SUMMER, HOW'S THE DAY CLINIC GOING?

IT'S OKAY, I SUPPOSE. I LIKE THE DOCTOR RUNNING IT.

ARE YOU EATING NORMALLY?

THE DOCTOR SAYS SOMETHING LIKE THIS CAN'T BE FIXED OVERNIGHT, BUT...I PUT ON A COUPLE OF POUNDS THIS WEEK...THAT'S GOOD, ISN'T IT?

WHAT ARE THE CUPCAKES FOR? GIANT PANDA? SIBERIAN TIGER? BLUE WHALE?

BRILLIANT!

A LOCAL PONY SANCTUARY.

I CAN'T TELL THEM EVERYTHING.

BY THE WAY, HONEY'S HOMEROOM TEACHER GAVE ME SOME WORKSHEETS FOR HER. SHE ASKED IF SHE WAS FEELING ANY BETTER--I DIDN'T KNOW WHAT TO SAY. SOMETHING STRANGE IS GOING ON.

SHOULD WE SAY SOMETHING? FORGET THE PACT THAT WE MADE WHEN WE WERE LITTLE...SOME THINGS SHOULDN'T STAY SECRET.

WE CAN'T TELL. WHAT WOULD WE SAY? AFTER THAT REPORT CARD, IT'D JUST LOOK LIKE WE WERE STIRRING UP TROUBLE.

WE HAVE TO TALK ABOUT IT WITH HONEY FIRST. COCO, YOU'RE THE YOUNGEST, SHE'LL LISTEN TO YOU MORE EASILY.

MAYBE, IF I GET THE CHANCE.

AROUND MIDNIGHT, I WAS MAKING A BANNER FOR THE CUPCAKE SALE WHEN HONEY GOT HOME, WITH HER LIPSTICK SMUDGED, HER HAIR RUMPLED. LAUGHING, I ASKED HER IF SHE'D SPENT THE EVENING AT ANTHONY'S STUDYING. SHE ASKED ME NOT TO TELL ON HER. SHE WAS SUPPOSED TO BE HOME BY 9 PM. I PROMISED I WOULDN'T TELL ON HER. I DIDN'T HAVE THE STRENGTH TO TALK TO HER ABOUT THE CLASSES SHE WAS SKIPPING. SOMEONE NEEDS TO TELL ON HONEY, AND SOON. IT JUST WON'T BE ME.

THE NEXT DAY DURING BREAKFAST...

YES, COME IN!

JUST A COURTESY CALL, SIR. WE'RE INVESTIGATING THE THEFT OF TWO PONIES THAT OCCURRED LAST WEEKEND.

≈SHPRITZ≈

IT'S POSSIBLE THE THIEVES ARE STILL IN THE AREA. WE'RE ADVISING RESIDENTS TO KEEP AN EYE OUT AND ALERT US OF ANY SUSPICIOUS INDIVIDUALS.

WE'LL LET YOU KNOW IF WE SEE OR HEAR OF ANYTHING UNUSUAL.

WILL YOU VISIT ME IN PRISON?

YOU BETCHA!

AT SCHOOL, DURING THE LUNCH BREAK...

ANOTHER BAKE SALE?

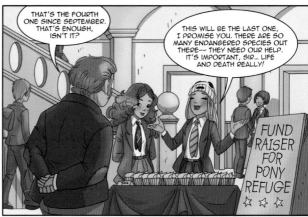

THAT'S THE FOURTH ONE SINCE SEPTEMBER. THAT'S ENOUGH, ISN'T IT?

THIS WILL BE THE LAST ONE, I PROMISE YOU. THERE ARE SO MANY ENDANGERED SPECIES OUT THERE-- THEY NEED OUR HELP. IT'S IMPORTANT, SIR... LIFE AND DEATH REALLY!

FUND RAISER FOR PONY REFUGE ☆ ☆ ☆

DON'T TOUCH IF YOU DON'T WANT TO BUY THE CAKE.

IT'S DARREN!

HEY!

WHATEVER. IF YOU CAN'T KID AROUND, I DON'T WANT YOUR CAKE!

LET GO OF ME!

YOU WERE THE ONE WHO HOISTED MY PANDA HAT UP THE OTHER DAY. AND YOU'RE THE ONE BOTHERING EVERYONE. HERE, YOU CAN HAVE MY CUPCAKE!

LEAVE THE LITTLE KIDS ALONE FROM NOW ON. NOBODY LIKES A BULLY, OKAY?

OKAY, OKAY!

LATER, AT THE COTTAGE...

WE HAVE ENOUGH TO BUY FEED FOR THE PONIES FOR A WEEK. I SOLD ALL MY CUPCAKES.

THAT'S GOOD. THANKS.

THE POLICE CAME TO OUR HOUSE THIS MORNING, WARNING US THAT HORSE THIEVES WERE IN THE AREA. I NEARLY FAINTED.

YEAH, IT'S NOT LIKE WE WERE INVOLVED IN A MURDER.

I'VE BEEN THINKING ABOUT THE PONIES AND I'VE COME UP WITH A PLAN.

I'LL KEEP CARAMEL. I'LL PUT HER IN THE BARN AT MY HOME.

I THINK YOU'VE FORGOTTEN SOMETHING. EVERYONE'S LOOKING FOR HER.

SOMETIMES, THE BEST PLACE TO HIDE SOMETHING IS RIGHT UNDER EVERYONE'S NOSES. THE POLICE WERE WARNING US TO LOOK OUT FOR THIEVES, NOT SEARCHING OUR BARN.

AND YOU COULD ASK YOUR PARENTS TO HIDE THE PREGNANT MARE.

YOU THOUGHT WRONG! FORGET IT!

DID I SAY SOMETHING I SHOULDN'T HAVE?

MY FAMILY IS COMPLICATED. DAD LEFT US A COUPLE OF YEARS AGO. WE HAVEN'T HEARD FROM HIM SINCE. AND MY MOTHER HAS ENOUGH PROBLEMS OF HER OWN RIGHT NOW.

LOOK, COCO, I CAN'T TALK ABOUT THIS.

OKAY, HERE. I SAVED TWO CUPCAKES FOR YOUR LITTLE SISTER.

SHE'LL LOVE THEM. THANKS!

OKAY, I HAVE TO GET HOME.

I'M AFRAID EVERYONE'S TALKING ABOUT THE HORSE THIEVES. I'M AFRAID OF GIVING MYSELF AWAY. I'M DREADING MY NEXT RIDING LESSON AND I HAVEN'T MANAGED TO APOLOGIZE YET TO JEAN AND ROY FOR RIDING CARAMEL WITHOUT PERMISSION. I'D MUCH RATHER BE HERE AT JASMINE COTTAGE.

IT'S CRAZY HOW STEVIE ACTS LIKE A WILD ANIMAL. HE'S SCARED, WITHDRAWN, BUT WHEN I GIVE HIM CUPCAKES FOR HIS SISTER, HE GETS ALL SWEET. HE'S A MYSTERY.

I'LL GO TO THE MUSIC CLASS ON FRIDAY INSTEAD OF GOING TO THE RIDING SCHOOL. THAT'S SAFER. I'LL WORK ON MY VIOLIN.

LATE SATURDAY MORNING...

I'D LOVE TO GO TO THE MOORS WITH CARAMEL.

SOMEBODY MIGHT SEE YOU AND, THEN, IF YOU END UP FALLING OFF HER AGAIN... IT'S RISKY!

THERE'S NOBODY. COME ON!

I WON'T DO ANYTHING TO SPOOK HER.

OKAY, WE'LL JUST GO INTO THE NEIGHBORING FIELD, BUT ON ONE CONDITION...

TEN MINUTES LATER...

I DON'T NEED ANYONE LOOKING OUT FOR ME. I CAN RIDE HER BY MYSELF.

IT'S THIS OR NOTHING!

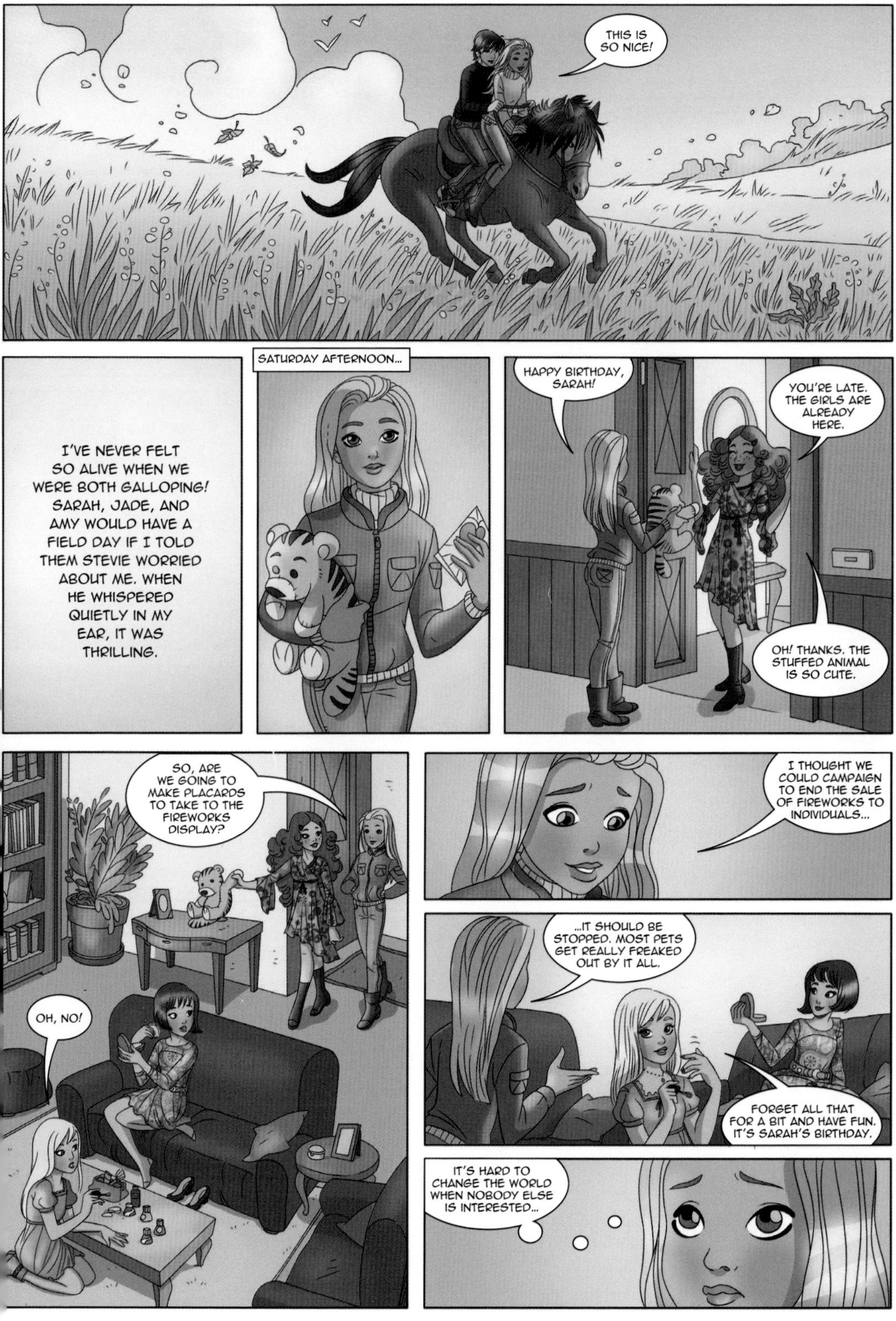
THIS IS SO NICE!
I'VE NEVER FELT SO ALIVE WHEN WE WERE BOTH GALLOPING! SARAH, JADE, AND AMY WOULD HAVE A FIELD DAY IF I TOLD THEM STEVIE WORRIED ABOUT ME. WHEN HE WHISPERED QUIETLY IN MY EAR, IT WAS THRILLING.
SATURDAY AFTERNOON...
HAPPY BIRTHDAY, SARAH!
YOU'RE LATE. THE GIRLS ARE ALREADY HERE.
OH! THANKS. THE STUFFED ANIMAL IS SO CUTE.
SO, ARE WE GOING TO MAKE PLACARDS TO TAKE TO THE FIREWORKS DISPLAY?
OH, NO!
I THOUGHT WE COULD CAMPAIGN TO END THE SALE OF FIREWORKS TO INDIVIDUALS...
...IT SHOULD BE STOPPED. MOST PETS GET REALLY FREAKED OUT BY IT ALL.
FORGET ALL THAT FOR A BIT AND HAVE FUN. IT'S SARAH'S BIRTHDAY.
IT'S HARD TO CHANGE THE WORLD WHEN NOBODY ELSE IS INTERESTED...

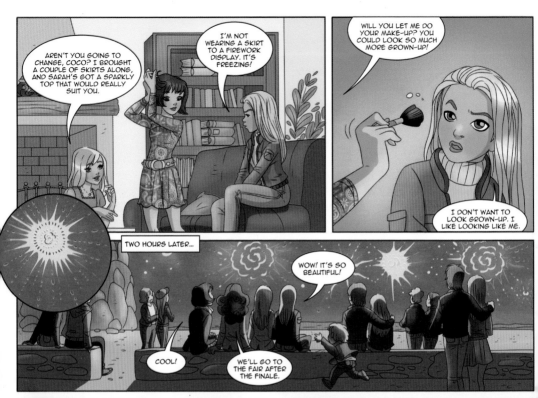

ARENT YOU GOING TO CHANGE, COCO? I BROUGHT A COUPLE OF SKIRTS ALONG, AND SARAH'S GOT A SPARKLY TOP THAT WOULD REALLY SUIT YOU.

I'M NOT WEARING A SKIRT TO A FIREWORK DISPLAY. IT'S FREEZING!

WILL YOU LET ME DO YOUR MAKE-UP? YOU COULD LOOK SO MUCH MORE GROWN-UP!

I DON'T WANT TO LOOK GROWN-UP. I LIKE LOOKING LIKE ME.

TWO HOURS LATER...

WOW! IT'S SO BEAUTIFUL!

COOL!

WE'LL GO TO THE FAIR AFTER THE FINALE.

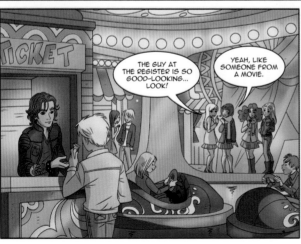

THE GUY AT THE REGISTER IS SO GOOD-LOOKING... LOOK!

YEAH, LIKE SOMEONE FROM A MOVIE.

TICKET

A FEW MINUTES LATER...

ISN'T THAT YOUR SISTER WITH THE CIRCUS GUY? THEY LOOK LIKE THEY REALLY GET ALONG.

YES, THAT'S HONEY. WHAT'S SHE DOING HERE? SHE'S NOT SUPPOSED TO BE GOING OUT.

THE NEXT DAY AFTER SCHOOL, INSPIRED BY STEVIE'S EXAMPLE, I DECIDE TO TAKE MY SCHOOLWORK UP TO THE COTTAGE TOO, WHERE WE NOW SPEND MOST OF OUR AFTERNOONS. HE HELPS ME WITH MATH AND, IN EXCHANGE, I HELP HIM WITH ENGLISH. I CATCH HIM WATCHING ME IN A WAY THAT MAKES MY CHEEKS BURN...

SO...HOW COME YOU DON'T STUDY AT HOME?

YOU DON'T KNOW WHAT IT'S LIKE AT HOME FOR ME. I'M TOO BUSY TO STUDY.

BUSY DOING WHAT?

LIKE LOOKING OUT FOR MY MUM AND SISTER. YOU'RE VERY NOSY, AREN'T YOU?

YOU'RE VERY SECRETIVE. WHAT ARE YOU, SOME KIND OF PRE-TEEN SPY? YOU DON'T MAKE IT EASY FOR ANYONE TO GET TO KNOW YOU.

GOOD. I'M NOT LOOKING FOR FRIENDS. I HAD THEM ONCE. "MOVE TO THE COUNTRY, START OVER," MUM SAID...IT'S BEEN A DISASTER FROM START TO FINISH.

THE ONLY GOOD THING ABOUT THE COUNTRYSIDE IS THE ANIMALS. THE PEOPLE ARE ROTTEN. BAD PEOPLE ALWAYS COME OUT ON TOP!

STEVIE? YOU CAN TALK TO ME, IF YOU HAVE PROBLEMS.

NO! I AM NOT ONE OF YOUR CHARITY PROJECTS.

LEAVE ME ALONE!

HE'S CRYING? I SAW TEARS.

MONDAY MORNING AT SCHOOL...

YOU'RE FAMOUS! OR INFAMOUS MAYBE...

SHHH! KEEP YOUR VOICE DOWN!

"REWARD OFFERED FOR STOLEN PONIES. TEN DAYS AGO, HEARTLESS THIEVES STOLE A SMALL GIRL'S BIRTHDAY PONY, LEAVING HER INCONSOLABLE... A MUCH-LOVED FAMILY PET."

ARE YOU SURE THEY WERE BEING MISTREATED?

OFFERING A REWARD IS BAD NEWS. PEOPLE WILL BE WATCHING OUT FOR THOSE PONIES NOW.

BETTER STEP UP THE SECURITY THEN, OR YOU'LL MAKE THE HEADLINES AGAIN!

AS THE YOUNGEST HORSE-THIEF IN THE WORLD!

DID YOU SEE HOW STEVIE LOOKED AT YOU? HE FANCIES YOU!

TOTALLY! ALL DARK AND SMOLDERING!

WHY DOES HE ALWAYS ACT AS THOUGH I DON'T EXIST AT SCHOOL?

HEY! WAIT FOR ME!

84

AFTER SCHOOL, AT TANGLEWOOD...

I'VE BEEN A FOOL. I'VE BEEN KIDDING MYSELF...SO WRAPPED UP IN BUSINESS I DIDN'T NOTICE WHAT WAS GOING ON RIGHT UNDER MY NOSE.

OH, NO! I'VE BEEN DISCOVERED!

MUM? WHAT IS IT?

WE'VE BEEN ASKED TO COME TO SCHOOL TO DISCUSS HONEY'S CONTINUED ABSENCES AND ERRATIC GRADES. BUT HER REPORT CARD WAS EXCELLENT...IT DOESN'T MAKE SENSE.

I WAS PROUD OF HER WHEN I SAW HER REPORT CARD...

SO, HONEY, TELL ME THIS ISN'T TRUE!

YOU'RE NOT ATTENDING CLASS ANYMORE?

IT'S A MISTAKE, OBVIOUSLY! THEY GOT THE WRONG STUDENT. YOU'VE SEEN MY REPORT CARD! AND ALSO, I TAKE THE BUS EVERY DAY WITH MY SISTERS.

RIGHT, SUMMER? SKYE? CHERRY? YOU MUST SEE ME IN THE CORRIDORS SOMETIMES. NO? ANSWER!

MY SISTERS HAVE NEVER LOOKED MORE UNCOMFORTABLE. IT'S TIME TO STOP COVERING UP FOR HONEY. I'M GLAD I'M NOT IN HIGH SCHOOL... THAT NOBODY ASKS ME.

HONEY'S BEEN EXPELLED FROM SCHOOL. MUM AND PADDY WENT IN TO SEE THE PRINCIPAL THIS MORNING, AND EVERYTHING CAME OUT. HONEY'S BEEN LYING FOR MONTHS. SHE WAS TAKING THE BUS TO GO TO SCHOOL, BUT SHE WAS DISAPPEARING OFF TO TOWN. TURNS OUT SHE'D MET THIS BOY WHO WORKS AT THE FAIRGROUND AND WAS HANGING OUT WITH HIM. BUT THE WORST THING IS, WITH THE HELP OF A GEEKY FRIEND, SHE MADE FAKE REPORT CARDS AND SENT FAKE DOCTOR'S NOTES TO THE TEACHERS. WORLD WAR THREE IS RAGING AT HOME.

THANKS FOR COMING, STEVIE!

WHAT'S GOING ON? I GOT YOUR TEXT AND WAS WORRIED.

MY FAMILY IS IN A CRISIS...AGAIN. MY MUM AND PADDY HAVE TO TALK WITH HONEY. SHE MAY HAVE TO GO TO SYDNEY TO LIVE WITH OUR DAD.

I NEEDED SOME AIR, TO LEAVE THE HOUSE, TO SEE CARAMEL. I'VE BEEN FORCED TO LIE LIKE HONEY. I'M NOT PROUD OF MYSELF. I SAID I WAS SLEEPING OVER AT SARAH'S.

YOU DON'T HAVE YOUR BIKE?

NO, I COULDN'T GO BACK BY THE HOUSE AFTER THE AUDITION...

WHAT AUDITION?

SINCE I'M NOT GOING TO THE RIDING SCHOOL ANYMORE, I WANTED TO DO MUSIC IN ITS PLACE. THERE WAS AN AUDITION TO BE PART OF THE SCHOOL ORCHESTRA, BUT I FAILED IT. APPARENTLY I SUCK AT IT.

A FEW MINUTES LATER...

EVERYONE THINKS WE'RE SO PERFECT, BUT WE'RE REALLY NOT! ⇒PFF!⇐

WE'VE HAD TO RUN A B&B IN OUR BIG HOUSE TO MAKE ENDS MEET. ONE OF MY SISTERS HAS AN EATING DISORDER, ONE'S IN LOVE WITH A GHOST, ONE SKIPS SCHOOL AND ONLY THINKS ABOUT BOYS, ADD A STEPSISTER WHOM MY SISTER HONEY CAN'T STAND BECAUSE SHE STOLE HER BOYFRIEND...

NEIGHH

THE PONIES, QUICK-- SOMETHING'S WRONG!

THE MARE-- SHE'S FOALING!

WHAT DO WE DO?

WE MUST LAY OUT HAY IN THE KITCHEN, MAKE A FIRE, AND HOPE FOR THE BEST.

HER WATER HAS BROKEN. DO YOU THINK IT'LL BE ALL RIGHT?

YOU COULD PLAY THE VIOLIN TO HELP HER!

I THINK SHE'S ALMOST THERE. I SEE THE FOAL'S LEGS.

A FEW MINUTES LATER...

WE COULD CALL HIM *STAR*. IT'S SUCH A CLEAR SKY TONIGHT, YOU CAN SEE WHOLE CONSTELLATIONS.

THIS FOAL IS SO BEAUTIFUL. I'M SO MOVED TO HAVE BEEN HERE FOR ALL THIS!

I'LL STAY HERE WITH YOU TONIGHT. WE MUST KEEP AN EYE ON THE MARE AND HER FOAL.

BUT THEY THINK I'M AT SARAH'S TONIGHT. WHAT ABOUT YOU?

I DON'T CARE! I'LL TELL YOU SOMETIME. MY LIFE IS SO COMPLICATED.

I HEARD SEDDON'S BOUGHT TWO MORE HORSES. IT DRIVES ME MAD. HE'S GOING TO MISTREAT THEM.

WE HAVE TO SAVE THEM, TOO!

WE CAN'T LEAVE THEM THERE! WE DON'T HAVE TO BRING THEM UP HERE, THAT WOULD ENDANGER CARAMEL AND SPIRIT AND STAR...

WE COULD TAKE THEM SOMEWHERE SAFE...LIKE THE RIDING SCHOOL PERHAPS... AND...I HAVE AN IDEA!

AT THE SAME TIME, WE COULD SEND A NOTE TO THE POLICE AND TO THE GAZETTE, ABOUT HOW SEDDON TREATS HIS ANIMALS.

IT COULD WORK. WE COULD TIP OFF THE POLICE AND THE NEWSPAPERS. MAYBE SOMEONE WILL ACTUALLY CHECK UP ON SEDDON AND FIND OUT WHAT HE'S REALLY LIKE.

AND THAT WAY, IF WE MANAGE TO PUT THE OTHER PONIES AT JEAN AND ROY'S, WITH THAT LETTER, IT'LL PROTECT EVERYONE AND IT WON'T BE THEFT.

MEET TOMORROW AT MIDNIGHT AT SEDDON'S!

AND I'LL DRAFT SOME LETTERS FOR THE POLICE AND THE NEWSPAPER.

THE FALLOUT IS STILL SETTLING WHEN I RETURN HOME ON SATURDAY MORNING. HONEY'S IN THE LIVING ROOM WATCHING OUR BAMBI DVD AND EATING CRUMPETS. SHE LOOKS UNBOTHERED, NOT LIKE SHE'S JUST BEEN EXPELLED FROM SCHOOL. MUM AND PADDY ARE IN THE KITCHEN. THEY LOOK SHATTERED. THERE'S A LUMP IN MY THROAT AS I FLOP DOWN BESIDE HONEY NOW...

YOU OKAY? ARE YOU GROUNDED AGAIN?

DON'T THINK SO. WHAT'S THE POINT? BESIDES, I'M OUT OF HERE.

YOU'LL ALL BE RID OF ME. SORRY TO DITCH YOU, LITTLE SIS, BUT I FINALLY GET TO ESCAPE THIS DUMP. I'M GOING OUT TO AUSTRALIA TO LIVE WITH DAD. THIS TIME NEXT WEEK, I'LL BE IN SYDNEY.

YOU CAN'T! WHAT ABOUT US?

YOU'VE MADE YOUR CHOICE. MUM MARRIED A LOSER. SHE PUTS HIM FIRST THE WHOLE TIME.

YOU'RE NOT BEING FAIR. MUM HAS DONE HER BEST TO HELP YOU, AND SO HAS PADDY.

PADDY'S NOT MY DAD, AND HE NEVER WILL BE! I MISS DAD.

WE ALL MISS HIM, EVEN IF HE FORGETS OUR BIRTHDAYS.

I'LL ONLY BE GONE FOR A FEW MONTHS. DAD'S FOUND A GOOD DAY SCHOOL THERE.

I REALLY HOPE THE DAY SCHOOL IS GOOD BECAUSE IF THINGS ARE LEFT TO DAD, HONEY WON'T BE ON THE EDGE FOR MUCH LONGER...SHE'LL TUMBLE RIGHT OVER IT AND GO INTO FREEFALL.

OKAY, WE'LL MEET AT SEDDON'S AT MIDNIGHT! I JUST DROPPED OFF THE LETTERS AT THE POLICE STATION AND NEWSPAPER.

WHAT DID YOU TELL YOUR PARENTS?

THAT I'M SPENDING THE NIGHT AT SARAH'S. THEY HAVE SO MUCH ON THEIR PLATE RIGHT NOW, THEY WON'T EVEN THINK OF CHECKING UP.

OPERATION RESCUE PONIES... HERE GOES!

WOOF!

SHEESH--I FORGOT ABOUT THE DOG. WAIT A MOMENT, COCO. I'LL BE BACK.

≥SHHHH!!≤

I HOPE NO ONE HEARD HIM!

WE'RE TAKING THE DOG, TOO. PLEASE, STEVIE. SHE LOOKS ILL-TREATED, TOO. SHE'S SO THIN.

ALL RIGHT, COME WITH US!

HIDE BEFORE HE SEES YOU!

BANG

THAT WAS A GUNSHOT... OH, MY GOD!

WHAT THE HELL ARE YOU DOING, STEVIE? LEAVE THE DOG BE AND GET IN THE HOUSE!

HOW DOES SEDDON KNOW STEVIE'S NAME?

I THOUGHT YOU WERE ONE OF THOSE BLASTED BURGLARS! WHAT ARE YOU DOING WITH THAT DOG? SHE'S NOT A PET, SHE'S A GUARD DOG!

WHAT'S THIS? DON'T TELL ME, A LITTLE RESCUE PARTY!

YOU TOOK THE OTHERS, TOO, DIDN'T YOU? TO SPITE ME! DIDN'T YOU, STEVIE, IS THAT IT? ANSWER ME!

YOU'RE A USELESS, PATHETIC EXCUSE FOR A BOY. I'VE TRIED TO TEACH YOU HOW TO HAVE A BACKBONE, HOW TO BE A MAN...

...BUT I CAN SEE MERE DISCIPLINE WON'T DO IT. YOU NEED TO BE BROKEN, JUST LIKE THE HORSES!

JAMES, WHAT'S GOING ON? SHALL I CALL THE POLICE?

IT'S STEVIE, MOMMY!

LEAVE HIM ALONE! LEAVE HIM ALONE, PLEASE!

THAT'S THE LITTLE GIRL I SAW CRYING THE LAST TIME? IS SHE STEVIE'S SISTER THEN?

BEFORE I CAN UNDERSTAND WHAT'S HAPPENING, SEDDON LASHES OUT, SLAPPING THE WOMAN SO HARD THAT SHE STARTS BLEEDING. IN THE GENERAL PANIC, THE PONY BUCKS AND REARS, CATCHING SEDDON ON THE TEMPLE, SO THAT HE REELS BACK AND FALLS TO THE GROUND. I TAKE LITTLE JASMINE BY THE HAND, HER MOTHER GETS UP, HELPED BY STEVIE. STEVIE GOES LOOKING FOR THE CAR KEYS. WE RACE ACROSS THE STABLE YARD TOWARDS THE FOUR-WHEEL DRIVE PARKED ON THE DRIVEWAY. AND WE DRIVE OFF IN THE DARKNESS, AWAY FROM THERE. TAKING THE SKINNY DOG, TOO...

IS--IS EVERYONE OKAY?

WE HAVE TO GO TO THE POLICE--WE HAVE NO CHOICE THIS TIME!

I CAN'T-- WE CAN'T--

THE PIECES OF THE PUZZLE ARE STARTING TO FIT TOGETHER...STEVIE HAS A LITTLE SISTER, A MOTHER, AND A VIOLENT STEPDAD...THAT'S WHY HE KNEW CARAMEL AND SPIRIT AND WHY HE HATES SEDDON SO MUCH. HE LIVES WITH HIM.

DRIVE TO MY PLACE. YOU'LL BE SAFE THERE!

A QUARTER OF AN HOUR LATER...

TELL ME WHAT HAPPENED!

STEVIE'S MY FRIEND FROM SCHOOL. WE WERE TRYING TO RESCUE SOME PONIES, AND IT ALL GOT OUT OF HAND...

WEREN'T YOU SLEEPING OVER AT SARAH'S?

WAY TO GO, LITTLE SIS! STEPPING INTO MY SHOES AS THE TROUBLEMAKER ALREADY? I HAVEN'T EVEN GONE YET!

HE HIT MY MUM. AND HE SHOT HIS GUN! I DON'T LIKE HIM. HE'S MEAN!

93

I CALLED THE POLICE. THEY'RE COMING!

SANDY, STEVIE'S MUM, ENDED UP TELLING US THE WHOLE STORY. THEY'D ALL THREE MOVED TO THE AREA. SANDY MET SEDDON, AND THAT'S WHEN EVERYTHING WENT BAD. HE WOULD HIT HER. STEVIE HAD TO STAND BY AND WATCH AS FEAR PULLED HIS FAMILY APART.

YOU AND I NEED A LITTLE TALK.

I'M GLAD YOU BROUGHT STEVIE AND SANDY AND JASMINE HERE, BUT...WHAT ON EARTH HAVE YOU BEEN THINKING? STEALING PONIES, LYING TO ME, WANDERING AROUND IN THE DARK? THAT WAS REALLY DANGEROUS.

SORRY, MUM, I JUST-- DIDN'T KNOW WHAT TO DO!

YOU COULD'VE TALKED TO ME. TOGETHER, WE COULD'VE WORKED SOMETHING OUT.

YOU REFUSED TO BUY CARAMEL FOR ME...

I TOLD YOU THAT WAS IMPOSSIBLE...

SWEETIE, I WANT YOU TO BECOME A LITTLE MORE REASONABLE. I ALREADY HAVE HONEY CAUSING ME WORRIES. SUMMER AND HER ILLNESS--SO STOP! I WANT YOU TO STOP YOUR FOOLISHNESS.

I WILL. I PROMISE. I'LL MAKE YOU PROUD OF ME.

A FEW DAYS LATER...

I DON'T WANT YOU TO GO. I WILL MISS YOU, STEVIE MARSHALL!

I'LL MISS YOU TOO, BUT IT'S FOR THE BEST, THOUGH, TO GO LIVE WITH MY GRANDPARENTS. THE FARTHER MUM IS FROM SEDDON THE BETTER.

WITHOUT YOU, I'D HAVE NEVER DARED STAND UP TO SEDDON. I LET MYSELF GET INVOLVED IN THIS BIG ADVENTURE WITH CARAMEL AND THE MARE. YOU GAVE ME HOPE. OKAY, AT FIRST, I THOUGHT YOU WERE A LITTLE BIT CRAZY.

I AM A LITTLE BIT CRAZY! HA HA!

WELL, YOU'RE PROBABLY MY BEST FRIEND. MAYBE EVEN MORE THAN A FRIEND...

YOU'RE MY BEST FRIEND, TOO, BUT... WELL, I DON'T THINK I'M READY FOR ANYTHING MORE RIGHT NOW. IS THAT OKAY?

I GUESS. I'LL WAIT. I'LL COME BACK ONE DAY WHEN WE'RE OLDER!

A WEEK AGO, WE TOOK HONEY TO THE AIRPORT TO CATCH HER FLIGHT TO SYDNEY. AND BEFORE STEVIE, HIS MOTHER, AND JASMINE LEFT FOR THE NORTH OF ENGLAND, JASMINE ENTRUSTED CARAMEL TO ME. SHE COULDN'T TAKE HER TO HER GRANDPARENTS'S HOME. I PROMISED HER I'D TAKE CARE OF HER PONY. SHE'LL COME SEE HER AGAIN DURING THE NEXT SCHOOL VACATION.

THE END

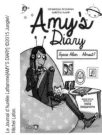

charmz chat

Welcome to SWEETIES #2 "Summer Coco," based on the Chocolate Box Girl series of novels by Cathy Cassidy, adapted by Véronique Grisseaux, writer, and Claudia & Marco Forcelloni, artists. We hope you enjoyed getting to really know Summer and Coco in this graphic novel, and Cherry and Skye in the first SWEETIES graphic novel. While these girls are now all part of the same family, it's clear they're all very different from each other.

Meeting each of the members of the Tanberry/Costello clan, it's easy to imagine them as "friends," even though they are fictitious characters. The same is true regarding the friendliness of the stars of other Charmz titles:

There's fourteen year old Amy Von Brandt, the star of AMY'S DIARY. Her diary is filled with scribbles about boy-craziness, best friends, cats, and possibly being from outer space. It's virtually impossible not to like Amy.

Chloe, a middle-schooler falling in and out of love, is the star of CHLOE. And we like her almost as much as her besties Mark and Fatou do.

G.F.F.s GHOST FRIENDS FOREVER involves a love triangle between paranormal investigator Sophia Greene-Camps, her ex-boyfriend Jake, and Whitney, an actual ghost. How cool would it be to have a friend who's a ghost-hunter or an actual ghost? (Skye can answer that one!)

Or imagine living in another time, and having a friend who is almost like a super-hero? In SCARLET ROSE, swashbuckling vigilante Maud must search for her father's killer while also figuring out where things stand with her masked crime-fighting partner, The Fox.

Or if you really want to get weird, check this Charmz series out: STITCHED. It's about Crimson Volania Mulch, a patchwork girl, who wakes up in a cemetery, soon to discover it's actually a lively place full of potential new relationships and friendships.

But that's not all. Coming soon to Charmz is someone we're sure you'll like: MONICA. She's had the same friends since she was little, but now their relationships are changing, just as they're changing and becoming teenagers. When Monica was little, she was the leader of her group of friends, and if any of them got out of line, she'd let 'em have it and wallop them with her plush bunny rabbit. Monica's main rival to lead her gang was Jimmy Five, who now prefers to be called "J-Five." He's matured to the point where being leader of the gang is no longer a priority, now he's focused on trying to make the planet a better place. Smudge is the one into sports, the more radical, the better. Maggy, is a caring friend that loves cats, and is into taking better care of her body. She focused on proper nutrition, exercise, and sports. Look for all of these new friends and more in MONICA ADVENTURES #1 "Who Can Afford the Price of Friendship Today?" and #2 "We Fought Each Other as Kids… Now We're in Love?!"

While the major theme tying all the Charmz graphic novels together is romance, friendship is a big factor in each title as well. Each Charmz graphic novel is almost like visiting friends and catching up with their lives. Whether their lives are close to ours (Amy, Chloe, Monica) or from another time (Maud) or even somewhat supernatural (Sophia and Crimson), what comes through in each series is that they all have the special qualities that we seek in choosing our friends. And that's why we all love spending time with them.

Speaking of which, don't miss SWEETIES #3 "Honey Cookie" coming soon, where we'll get know more about the eldest Tanberry sister and her step-brother.

Thanks, Jim

STAY IN TOUCH!

EMAIL: salicrup@papercutz.com
WEB: www.papercutz.com
TWITTER: @papercutzgn
FACEBOOK: PAPERCUTZGRAPHICNOVELS
REGULAR MAIL: Charmz, 160 Broadway, Suite 700,
                East Wing, New York, NY 10038

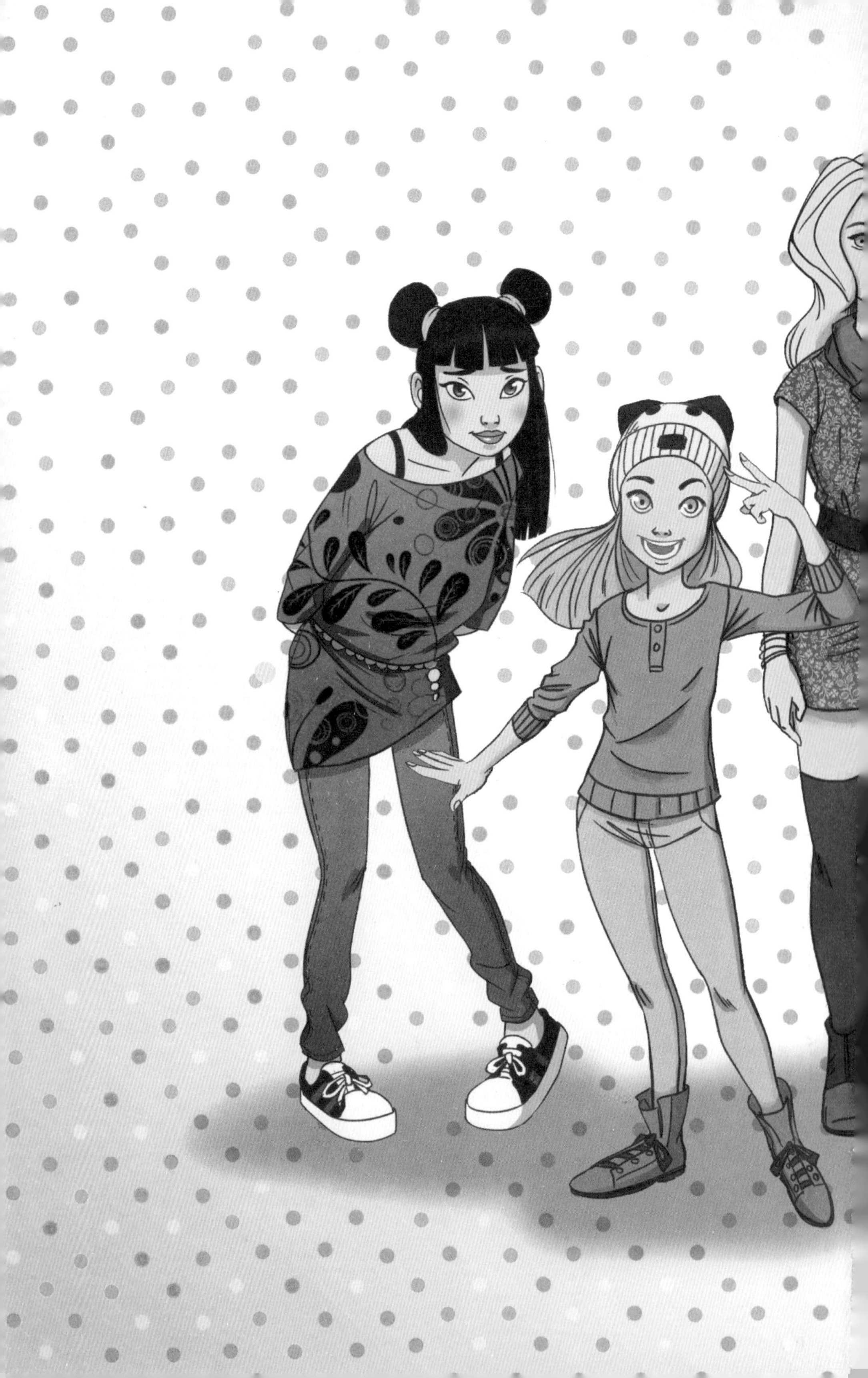